Bad Boy

Big City Billionaires

USA TODAY Bestselling Author
Nora Flite

Copyright © 2016 Nora Flite

All rights reserved. BILLION DOLLAR BAD BOY is a work of fiction. Names, characters, places, and incidents either are the product of the author's imagination or are used fictitiously. Any resemblance to actual persons, living or dead, events, or locales is entirely coincidental.

ISBN-13: 978-1530705085

ISBN-10: 1530705088

- Chapter 1 -
Alexis

The package that tumbled out of my mailbox was not addressed to me.

In fact, it wasn't addressed to *anyone*.

Brown paper, a simple glint of tape on the seams; it was as ordinary as possible. I mean, as ordinary as mystery boxes go.

Logically, I poked it with my shoe to make sure it wasn't dangerous somehow. You hear about it all the time on the news, packages that just explode or carry poison or something. Arsenic? Wasn't that the big thing recently?

My box didn't explode. It just rolled limply onto one side.

What the hell? I wondered silently, crouching down to get a closer look. Had someone sent me a package but forgotten to label it? That by itself was weird, *I* never got anything in the mail. Nothing besides bills, anyway.

"Are you alright?" The speaker was a sweet, older woman. She was decked out in the familiar slate-grey of a postal office employee. Though she was smiling at me, her eyes had that distinct 'I think you might be a crazy person, please leave right away' accusation in them.

Clearing my throat, I scooped up the box anxiously. "Uh, I'm fine. Just a little surprised." *That's an understatement.* "Sorry if I caused a scene."

The woman lifted her eyebrows, increasing my discomfort. A quick scan around the room revealed that the everyone was eyeballing me. I was probably the most exciting thing they'd seen all day.

Sweat crept down my neck; I'm not a fan of being the center of attention. Self-consciously, I tucked the box under my arm. It was about the size of a baseball, it fit perfectly against my ribs. "Again, really sorry—I'll uh, I'll just get out of your hair," I said.

Shutting my mailbox, I locked it quickly. Then, I used every ounce of strength I had to walk slowly through the front doors. The distance felt longer than a mile.

Climbing into my tiny, far-too-beaten-up Volkswagen, I breathed in deeply. The metal bubble was a perfect place to regain my composure.

Pushing the back of my skull into my seat, I closed my eyes.

This was an odd start to my day.

Speaking of odd...

Sitting up, I lifted the small box into view. It weighed as much as a kiwi, and when I turned it, I heard something rustle inside. Digging at the taped sides, I frowned. *Just what are you hiding in—*

A horn honked loudly; the box fumbled in my lap. Twisting around, I spotted a car behind me in the tiny lot. "Alright, alright! I'm going, chill out." Reluctantly, I set my package on the passenger seat. Clutching my keys, I started the engine, reversing to give the rude driver my parking space.

He shot me the stink-eye as we passed.

It wasn't a long trip back to my rent-a-home, but the entire time, my mind ran wildly with ideas. The contents of the box could be anything: nail polish, batteries, a dead goldfish.

Money.

Money would be nice, I mused soberly.

It didn't take a detective to realize I was running up against the poverty wall. My car was junk—it broke down constantly—and my home was nothing to brag about.

Pulling up to the yellowed front yard, something scrambled in the dumpster before vanishing into the shadows. It wasn't even noon and animals were in my trash.

The area was empty, just some skinny trees and another house or two, cracked streets and the occasional stray cat. Still, it was better than nothing.

Turning off the Volkswagen, I gathered my things and strode to my front door. The tiny house had been my home for five years. I'd moved in soon after high school.

For a while, I'd dreamed of going off to college in another city, or of traveling the world.

Dreams aren't very reliable.

Shoving the door open, I dropped my purse on the coffee table. Then I did a quick, paranoid check, making sure my home was empty.

You could never be too sure.

Breathing out, I dropped onto my couch, finally alone with the box.

"Reveal your secrets," I said to myself. I wanted to ease the tension.

It didn't work.

Fidgeting, I peeled the tape away. The box split, and when I tipped it, a small bag fell into my lap. Blinking, I stroked the luxurious material. Intrigued, I loosened the knot, carefully spilling the contents out onto my hand.

In the pale light of my single ceiling bulb, the earrings glinted like freshly poured silver. *Were* they silver? The emerald centers were bigger than acorns, so rich and deep I could have lost myself if I stared too long.

I didn't handle—or own—much jewelry, but even I could tell that these were expensive.

What... what the hell?

Entirely lost, I hefted the earrings, enjoying their weight. They were meant for a queen, not a girl who had holes in all of her jeans. There was no denying it, this gift was clearly *not* for me.

Chewing the side of my tongue, I set the earrings on my coffee table. The mystery of this was making me nervous. Wasn't it illegal to open mail not sent to you, a federal crime or something?

My eyes darted to the velvet satchel again. Putting the box aside, I dug into the bag. My fingertips brushed a hard edge. Eagerly, I tugged a piece of paper into view.

It was crisp, heavy card stock. My heart was doing its best impression of a drum-line as I opened the note. Curled, handwritten ink rolled before me.

The note was short, and I read it with prickles sprouting along my spine.

Dear Pet,

I hope you enjoy these. I'm picturing them now, clasped on your lovely ears, just begging for me to stroke them and make you whimper.

The green will draw every eye to you... but won't they be jealous, once they realize you're already claimed?

—S

I breathed in sharply—I'd forgotten I needed air.

Pet? S?

No, this was all a mistake. The wrong address, for sure. The earrings were for someone worth courting, and unless I was crazy, the vibe of the letter *screamed* 'sex' and 'kink.'

My life experiences pushed me far out of the kinky club. Hell, almost out of the sex club, too. Though I was twenty-three, I hadn't been in a serious relationship in forever—a fact my lovely mother liked to remind me of each time we spoke. Virgin? Oh, no. But I was close, and if it was possible to become one again, the way your piercings sometimes grew back over?

I'd be a virgin reborn by now.

Puffing air through my lips, I sank into my couch. The earrings taunted me, reminding me of everything I didn't have. Whoever this 'Pet' was, she had a rich admirer. *But good for her*, I mused sullenly. *She's probably a hot, confident girl to draw this kind of attention.*

The last guy I went out with tried to hold my hand at the end of the night.

I'd run away like a freak and never called him back.

My co-worker, Laralie, had set me up with the guy. When she heard that I slammed my door in his face, she'd thrown a magazine at me. She kept telling me to take initiative... to be more trusting, less scared of the world.

It was impossible to explain to her why I couldn't do that.

People say your scars heal with time. I think they just grow deeper, like tree roots.

Shaking myself, I reached for the jewelry. I froze in mid-movement, dropping my hands to squeeze my knees and drum my fingers.

Was it terrible that I wanted to hold the earrings again? Just to feel them?

It wasn't *so* bad, right?

Glancing around, as if someone could see inside my apartment, I groaned. *Don't be so pathetic. Just put everything in the box and...* My thoughts ended abruptly. What *was* I supposed to do? There was no return address, no way to send this gift off to the right person.

I didn't even know how it had gotten in my mailbox. Could you send mail without an address? Did someone at the post office mess things up, sticking this package in my locker and calling it a day?

There were so many questions that I had. One of them chewed at me extra fiercely:

I wonder how the earrings would look on me?

Slapping my cheeks quickly, I jumped to my feet. "Nope," I said to the room. "I'm not doing that. Bad idea. Think about something else." Spinning, I paced across the scratched up floorboards.

On the one hand, I could just *keep* the gift, but that felt all kinds of shady. On the other hand... doing the right thing was pretty impossible. Tomorrow, I'd just have to ask the people at the post office which of them had put the gift in my mail slot. Surely, *someone* had seen this 'S' or whoever.

If I reasoned it out, I could picture the scenario. The mystery man had gone to the counter, asked to have the box put in someone's locker... and the worker had slipped up and put it in mine, instead of this 'Pet' person's.

Breathing out, I slumped where I stood. It made so much sense. Not only that, but it gave me a solution.

Turning, I scooped up the earrings and dumped them in the bag, then added it and the letter to the box. My re-taping was a little shoddy, but it would suit.

By tomorrow, I'd be able to walk away from this mess.

- Chapter Two -

Alexis

"Hello again," I said brightly. I pushed the box onto the counter, meeting the eyes of the female employee from yesterday.

Her frown said she remembered me.

"This might sound weird," I said, "But someone accidentally put this into my mail." I nudged the box again. "Could you take this and deliver it to who it was meant for?"

She lowered her eyebrows, pursing her lips for a long minute. "If you want something delivered, it needs an address on it."

"No, I know that." Waving my hands side to side, I tried to look friendlier. "I'm saying someone put this *in my mail,* when it doesn't even *have* an address."

The woman, whose name tag read 'Betty,' squinted closer at the little box. "Huh. Well that's not standard practice at all."

Nodding patiently, I tapped the counter with emphasis. "Right! Standards. So someone who works here took this from some guy, and then put it in the wrong place."

"Wait," Betty said, locking a dubious stare onto me. "How do you know the sender was a guy if there's no name or anything on here?"

Red, molten shame burrowed into my guts. "Uh." *Fuck. Now she starts paying attention, great.* "Well, okay, so the thing is... because there *was* no name on it, I opened it, thinking maybe it was meant for me."

Betty's mouth curled into a deeper frown.

Perspiration blossomed on my chest. "I mean, easy mistake to make. It was in my mail! But inside, there was a note, which I read—and it obviously was sent from a man and meant for someone else and... and..."

18

Firmly, Betty put her hand on the box. "You opened it."

I swallowed. "Yeah."

"You do know that's a crime, ma'am?"

Every inch of my face was glowing. "But—well."

"*And* you expect me to take it back and magically figure out who it was meant for?"

I was at a loss. Tense as a fishing line, I clenched my hands at my hips. "...Yes?"

Deflating, the postal worker gave me a tired once-over. Then, she pushed the box back to me. "Honey, I don't know what to tell you. I don't have time to play cop *or* investigator. There's no name on here, it was in your mail, you opened it. Just keep the darn thing."

My mouth was slack. On reflex, I retrieved the package. Betty spared me one more look, then waved over my shoulder. "Next in line."

In a fog, I walked away from the counter. This wasn't how I'd expected things to go. What was I supposed to do with these earrings? Keeping them felt wrong, trashing them—jeez, they probably cost more than six months of my rent.

Amazingly, I found myself in front of my locker again. Peeking at Betty, I was tempted to set the box on the floor. Would this 'Pet' person see it, and know it was meant for her? I didn't know if this was the first gift or the millionth, a box was a box.

Shaking my head, I resolved to think of a new plan. I didn't have one yet, but in time, something would click.

It just had to.

Soothed by my rationalization, I slid my key into my mailbox. I was on autopilot, I checked my mail every morning if work wasn't in the way.

Yes. A new plan. Okay.

The tiny door swung open, hanging on its hinges and revealing the inside of my locker. My lungs hitched, ribs freezing. Everything became a far away dream.

No. Not again.

In front of me sat another box.

****

The gifts continued to arrive over the next two weeks.

Nothing I did could get them to stop; not talking to the postal workers, not asking for information on the deliveries, and not waiting around a whole day in my car to try and catch the mysterious S.

I'm not proud of that last one, but it's not like I wasted my *whole* day.

Besides, I had something else to feel guilty over.

I'd opened all of the boxes.

Not at first, no. I'd waited a few days before I cracked, the packages sitting on my kitchen counter. They were like nagging, loose threads on a fancy shirt, just waiting to be yanked.

I looked for ways to justify it, digging deep to wave away the wrongness of opening someone else's mail. I'd asked myself, *What can I do?* Hadn't I tried to make it right?

Gradually, I started looking forward to them. It wasn't even the gifts that excited me, it was those damn letters! They came in every box, always meticulously written and *soaking* with erotic tension.

He'd say things like, "I'm imagining how you'll gasp when I smell this perfume on your throat," or, "This color will match perfectly with your lips, once they're red and swollen with desire."

S knew how to keep my attention.

Progressively, the gifts began to get more personal. The earrings were almost innocent when held up against the Jimmy Choo pumps (how did Pet and I wear the same size?) or the Sferra Milos sheets.

Then the lingerie appeared.

As I sat on my couch and lifted the creamy, decadently over-priced bustier, panties, and garter belt—something I'd never even *seen* in person before—into the air, I was stunned. The matching lace-topped hosiery completed the set.

Quickly, I peeled open the letter he'd sent to me—I mean, to Pet.

I had to remind myself of that.

Dear Pet,

I saw this outfit on a mannequin. I knew it would look far better on you.

I'm tempted to give you my phone number, just so you can send me a photo of you wearing the lingerie.

Another time, maybe.

For now, wear it for me, and when you do, I want you to imagine me standing there, watching. Close your eyes and think how wonderful my fingers will feel as they graze across the smooth silk.

How sensitive it will make your skin.

How hard your nipples will become.

It'd take so very little to tempt you further. You'd moan and squirm while I brought you so close to coming. In time, you'd be begging me to get you off.

Wouldn't that be fun?

I'll leave you with that thought.

Next time, my surprise for you will be even more delicious.

—S

I realized I'd been clutching the letter.

My heart was in my throat, swelling beyond belief as the rest of me struggled to figure out how to feel. The letters had always been intense, clearly private, but this... this was straight up obscene!

Shifting on the couch, I shivered at the movement. Reading his words had called up vivid images, setting my skin aflame even under my boring jeans and t-shirt.

Okay. Just take a breath and relax. Setting the letter down, I glanced immediately at the lingerie. I'd gotten the impression from his writing that S *had* met Pet, but maybe I was wrong. They had to be in contact somehow though, right?

He said she doesn't have his number.

Too much of this was still a mystery.

Part of me was glad he hadn't handed over his phone number. It meant I wasn't tempted to do what he'd said; take a photo in the outfit and—*Stop*, I chastised myself. *You know that's wrong, plus you wouldn't have the guts. Besides, if you had his number, you could finally explain the mix up.*

Yes. Of course.

Then everything would go back to normal.

Smoothing my hair back, I sighed. *Boring, but normal.* Why did that feel so depressing suddenly? I wanted to stop the packages, or...

I thought I did.

Peering at the lingerie, I chewed my lip. *This is a dangerous game.* S could be anybody, *Pet* could be anybody. I was getting too deep into their little world, it wasn't meant for me. I should have thrown everything in the trash, or at least never opened the boxes.

Why was resisting so hard?

My heart thumped, and finally, I reached for the bustier.

Under my palms, it was cool and luxurious. Helplessly, I rubbed it on my cheek. *How much did this cost?* I'd never gone inside a fancy lingerie store, just seen the occasional expensive bra while browsing the sale items at my local outlet mall.

As I breathed in the clean scent of the material, I pictured—or tried to picture—this S as he shopped. Had he gone past the display window, then turned back for a closer look? Had he been out deliberately looking for lingerie?

And... and what would it feel like, wearing this? Having him see me in it, aching to touch me while I longed to be touched? A shudder rolled down to my toes.

Standing, I hurried to my bedroom.

Don't do this, I told myself. It was futile; I already had my jeans around my ankles. Tossing my plain clothes aside, I eagerly slid the bustier over my head. Every place it touched brought bliss. My cells woke with excitement.

Whatever resistance I had vanished. It was as if the lingerie was pouring over my skin, milk into a glass, a thick coating that made my tongue tingle and my eyes flutter. It drifted over my hips, tickling my flesh.

It took me a second or two to figure out the garters, but when I did, I was delighted. They held the lace-topped leggings in place, the silk encasing my thighs tightly. It was an intimate embrace, stroking my arousal.

Peeling the panties upwards, I couldn't help but imagine they were being tugged onto me by someone else. Someone with calm, controlling muscles... someone who knew what he wanted and was determined to show me.

When the panties cupped my pussy, I breathed out sharply. My pulse went into overdrive. I was doing exactly what he'd said.

That thrilled me in a way I couldn't describe. I was peering into a perverse new world.

Catching a glimpse of myself in my full-length mirror, I froze.

The person looking back wasn't me. She was elegant, flaring with heat and eager to be touched. This was no shrinking, mousy girl, this...

This is wrong.

Blushing, I hurried to take everything off. I fumbled with the garters, toppling onto my bed in my panic. *Get it all off!* The backs of my eyes throbbed. *Why did I think this was okay?*

Every piece of clothing crumpled to the rug. Breathing heavily, I let the clean air rake over my naked skin. I'd been sweating, hot from the inside of my core.

In the mirror, I saw the confusion in my wide eyes. Yes. This girl looked more like me.

Baffled, lost.

Pathetic.

Ruffling my hair, I eyed the outfit as if it was made of acid. It had felt *so good* to wear it, but the fantasy wasn't meant for me. Dipping into this private world that existed between two strangers, it was horrible.

As I hugged myself tight, flooding with shame over my actions, I couldn't deny the other feeling inside of me. Something crisp and wild that grew day by day.

Even if I knew this was wrong, and even if I admonished myself for going so far...

I anticipated the next gift more than ever.

- Chapter Three -
Alexis

"Those are lovely earrings."

My head snapped up, fingers touching my ears reflexively. Against the soft pads of my fingertips, the silver edges felt like barbed wire.

I knew I shouldn't have worn them, I just... I couldn't resist. I'd gotten so bad at controlling my impulses these days.

"Thanks," I mumbled, forcing a smile.

The cashier nodded, perhaps noticing my unease—perhaps not. "Where did you get them?"

My heart stopped. "Uh." *What do I say?* "Well..." *Shit shit shit.* Her question was innocent, but it forced me to remember how awful I was behaving. Where had I gotten these earrings?

I could never explain.

"They were a gift," I mumbled, face red and hot.

"Oh, lucky you," she chuckled. "Someone is generous."

My smile was brittle. "Yeah. Right."

She finished bagging my groceries, and I was just as quick to pay and leave.

Stupid, I told myself, tossing the food into my car's backseat. *You should have known better than to wear these out. Or to wear them at all!*

Settling into the car, I looked in my rear view mirror. This jewelry, it drew every eye— just like S had said it would. Once upon a time, I hadn't been so nervous about standing out in a crowd. It's funny how things change.

Or what changes us.

Don't think about that. You can't go down that road.

The past is a painful, vulnerable place. I preferred to avoid it.

I started the car, then paused. None of the gifts I kept receiving belonged to me. Never mind how illegal it was that I was opening these packages, what about all the moral codes I was breaking?

Setting my jaw tight, I pulled the earrings off and put them in my cup-holder. Removing them made me feel both lighter... and somehow more deflated.

This has to end. No more playing around. It didn't matter if I liked the gifts, my reality was clear as ice; none of this generosity was meant for me.

Playing pretend had to end. I couldn't return the gifts, but I didn't have to take them home with me. No one could force me to be involved in this whole mess.

I'm in control of my life. I need to remember that. I turned my radio up louder. Crushing the wheel, I steered my car towards my house. *I don't have to be so passive!*

33

Yes. I could do this.

I could turn the gifts away.

Who the hell was going to stop me?

I dropped my groceries off at home, checking the time as I did so. *Need to hurry and get to work.* Untangling my hair, I headed into my bedroom to find a change of clothes. Flipping through the racks of basic blouses and pants, I slid the hangers sideways.

In the far corner of my closet, a flash of red called to me. Briefly, I eyed the dresses that hung in the shadows. It was amazing that I had kept those for so long. They were from another time.

Quickly, I snatched an opal colored blouse and long skirt from the closet. Safe and bland—it was appropriate for my office job. Hoisting the clothing high, I twisted around. My toe caught in the mess on my floor, nearly tripping me.

Scowling, I straightened and eyed my unorganized bedroom. I *really* needed to clean up. Scanning the small space, my attention fell on the full laundry basket, the half-open wardrobe, the cluttered floor.

And then I saw it.

Shivering, I eyeballed the lingerie with both envy and unease. The silky material was flooding me with too many emotions. I couldn't bury the delicious memory from just the other night of how it had felt to wear the outfit.

Inching forward, I hesitated. *No. Don't do this.* My fingers clenched in the air. *Think about what you decided. Did you forget so easily?*

Right. My decision.

Gritting my teeth, I snatched up the lingerie with clawed fingers. Then, I stomped out of the room, not slowing until I shoved the beautiful clothing into my kitchen trash. When it was out of my grip, I leaned on the counter, breathing heavily.

I was proud of myself.

I also couldn't shake the cloying sensation that I'd wasted something wonderful.

No. I lifted my chin high. *This is how it has to be.*

Seeing the lingerie had nearly spiraled me into trying it on again. Or, at least, made me want to hide it in my dresser and never lose it.

Pushing a hand to my chest, I endured my throbbing heart. My abrupt laughter startled me. *Am I that worked up over this? I'm ridiculous.* I'd turned a small problem into a huge deal.

My mother would have called me dramatic.

And maybe she'd have been right.

Glancing at the clock, I winced. *And now I'm going to be late for work. Great.*

Stripping quickly, I pulled on my plain outfit and scrambled out the front door.

****

I managed to bury myself in work for the next few days.

It was easy enough; the place was buzzing as we prepared for a new magazine launch, and I had loads of papers to catch up on. For a little while, my mind was free from stress.

By the time I finally got the courage to return to the post office, it was Thursday. I'd never gone so long without checking my mail, but I just couldn't handle the anxiety over what I might find.

In the end, my nerves about forgotten bills or other important documents forced my hand.

Pushing into the tiny, faded building, I side-eyed my locker with growing unease. But this had to be done. *Just get it over with.* I couldn't keep hiding from my own mailbox forever. What an idea.

Steeling myself, I gripped the handle, slid my key inside, and cracked the door gently. Unfortunately, the pressure of the contents finally being freed meant that no matter how quiet I tried to be, the boxes and papers still exploded to the floor.

I shouted, stepping back with a wince. Not surprisingly, every customer stared my way.

I was becoming the local clown.

The packages spilled like rain; angry, bloated rain. In just five days, S had stuffed my locker with an assortment of presents.

A gangly young man in a postal uniform came my way. His brow was knotted, eyes darting from me, to the mess, and back again. "Are you alright?"

On reflex, I shook my head side to side. Then I cleared my throat. "Uh, fine. Just fine." I motioned helplessly at the boxes. "I didn't expect so much mail."

"That's not all of it," he said, flinching at my wild eyes. Nodding towards the counter, he shrugged. "Couldn't keep shoving it inside. There's a bin in the back with about four more packages. Want me to—"

"No." I cut him off, wiping my sweaty palms on my pants. "No, I don't want any of it. In fact, I'd like you..." I stared at his name tag. "Kerie—or whoever else—to stop putting unaddressed mail in my locker."

Kerie scratched the side of his neck. "What should we do with all of it?"

Gathering up the mess, I grunted as I stood. "Throw it out. That's what I'm doing, anyway." I turned, shuffling out of the building with great strides.

Approaching the dumpster out back, I threw everything into it with a grunt. The boxes rattled inside, joining the refuse. I was tired of being responsible for someone else's game.

Hopefully, he'd get the message that he had the wrong target. S needed to find his original play-thing, whoever she was.

Dusting my hands off, I walked to my car and glorified in my decision to get out of this weird pen-pal exchange. Was it really pen-pal, if I could never reply?

Would I have replied?

Biting my tongue, I jumped into my car and fled the scene. I drove as if everything might explode behind me, some violent fireball from an action movie.

I'd made my choice.

No one could stop me.

Not even *him*.

- Chapter Four -

Alexis

Monday arrived, just as wet as the rest of the weekend had been.

The rain had been coming down all morning. I'd been smart enough to bring an umbrella, the purple material turning slick from the downpour. Even so, as I darted across the parking lot and into my workplace, I couldn't avoid the puddles.

Observing my soaked ankles and flats in dismay, I hurried through the doors and sighed. Did that dumb orange cat really have to be right about Mondays?

The downtown building was large, brushing the clouds where it stood. Inside, multiple businesses rented sections for their own purposes. The tiny plaque inside the elevator indicated my destination—the twentieth floor.

Fixing my frizzy hair, I stepped into the publishing house of Salvador and Goldheart.

The wide room was a crisp eggshell color, dotted with overly green plants; most were fake. The soft hum of people flipping papers or talking about current projects was a constant white noise.

If I looked closely, I could see many of my fellow employees were half-asleep in their chairs. We ran the fashion magazine known as Velcro. I mean, as a secretary, I didn't exactly run much of anything. Not my dream job... but it kept me busy, and it helped pay my bills. What else mattered?

"Oh, Alexis!" Laralie was dressed in her usual style; tight black hose, red pumps, and a skirt that hugged her curves in a way I envied. She eyed my muddy ankles pointedly. "Still raining?"

Grinning good-naturedly, I shook my umbrella out. She stepped back, making sure she didn't get splattered. "Yeah," I said. "Still pretty wet. What's going on?"

Running her fingers through her short, angular black hair, she nodded over her shoulder. "You've got to come see! You're a little late, but I'm sure there are some left."

"Some left? Some of what?" Draping my coat on the back of my chair, I glanced at the phone. I was relieved nothing blinked at me; no missed calls. "I should really get to work, Mr. Salvador will lose his mind if he doesn't see me sitting here when he shows up."

"He's already here." She ignored my look of fright. Beaming, she gripped my elbow and tugged. "Just come on! Some food would be good for you. Unless you already ate?"

On cue, my stomach rumbled. "This is about food? Alright, you win." I *hadn't* eaten breakfast, so if there was something waiting for me, how could I turn it down?

Following her through the office, we took a sharp turn into the backroom. It was where we ate our lunches if we decided not to brave the busy streets of downtown Portland.

Laralie was blocking my view, so I couldn't see what was resting on the round table. I did spot the three other women who were hanging out and chatting, their hands gripping what looked like paper liners.

The vanilla scent was hitting me hard, my stomach cramping with hunger. I realized what they were eating; cupcakes. "Is it someone's birthday?"

Trying to make room for me to pass, Laralie said, "Don't think so. No one's sure who brought them."

"What?" I asked. "I don't get it, how can no one know—" My words died on my tongue.

Stuffed inside a large pink box were five cupcakes. There had clearly been more, but even with the empty spots, the display looked decadent.

They were squat, fat little things topped by metallic frosting. I'd never seen such beautiful designs on a cupcake before. The paper wrappings glowed, brilliant as moonlight.

On top of every cupcake was a small, elegant letter S.

"Don't they look beautiful?" someone said. It was hard to hear them, my ears felt swamped with water.

"Alexis?"

In a daze, I looked over to find Laralie staring at me. Her pretty blue eyes were wide with concern. "Alexis, are you okay? You look pale. Here, eat something!"

She offered me a cupcake, and I nearly slapped it from her grip. "Sorry!" I stammered, hands held high. "I don't—I mean—" My skull was pulsing, pushing my eyes forward so they bulged.

Laralie frowned, lowering the cupcake. "Maybe you should get some air."

Grabbing the door-frame, I nodded. "Yes. Air. Right." With a nervous look at everyone watching me, I darted out of the room. My flats were damp; I slipped on the tiles, grabbing onto the wall to stay upright.

Calm down! Just relax!

But how could I?

It was one thing to find mistaken packages in my mailbox. Here, where I worked... what did it mean?

Laralie was right, I needed air. I needed to *think*. None of this made sense. S must have noticed I wasn't taking the gifts, which I'd wanted. But instead of giving up and finding the right person's address, he'd sent something here.

But it's not meant for me. It isn't. It just can't be.

The elevator 'dinged.' The doors spread, but I didn't step inside. *The cupcakes are for someone else.* I kept clinging to that as a fact. And since it had to be true, it meant one of my coworkers was Pet!

The idea left my stomach in knots. I'd expected relief, but instead, I wasn't sure how to feel. Holding my temples, I chuckled—a tired, exasperated release. *I am so ridiculous. This isn't about you.*

Latching onto the idea that S was trying to get in touch with someone else—someone who just happened to work here—gave me a funny feeling. I felt less pressure.

I also felt a gnawing sensation around my heart.

The reality was this; no one would ever go to such lengths for me. Not boring, plain, keeps-to-herself Alexis Willow. I was a nobody, and nobodies slid under the radar.

I'd made sure of that.

S was after someone in my office. His options were bountiful. Laralie was gorgeous and fun, Heather was a blonde from Editing that had our male coworkers swooning. Even Denise, who mostly sat in on meetings and just nodded, like she was important, was worthy of a secret admirer.

Yes, I thought, crossing the room towards the solitary, wide desk that belonged to me. *Sometimes a coincidence is just that.* Sliding into my chair, I gave a half-spin, working so hard to ease my mood. *Smile,* I told myself. *Cheer up, stop moping.* Life was normal—my kind of normal. Boring and dull, but safe.

Safe was what I was looking for.

As I faced the room, settling in to check my email, my eyes caught something glinting.

It drew me down, yanked at my center until my stomach was flipping, my mouth dry and electric.

Impossible.

I told my brain this, but it didn't matter.

On my desk sat a single cupcake.

Beneath it was a letter.

Swallowing, I slid the paper into view. The surface was smooth, a single word scrawled, hidden by the sweet treat: Pet.

Blushing, I lifted my head, eyeing the room. Had anyone seen this? *No. Laralie would have mentioned it.* She was nosy, so if *she* had said nothing...

Biting my tongue, I worked the envelope open. Inside, the same brand of paper I'd touched several times waited for me. It shone in the overhead lights.

Pet,

If you want this to end, the choice is yours. Throw out my next gift, and I'll bring this to a close.

Enjoy the cupcake.

—S

Shutting my eyes, I hung my chin low. The note was the first real evidence that made something abundantly clear. Something I'd denied again and again and again.

The gifts *were* meant for me!

Gripping my skirt, I pushed my shoulders into my ears. My muscles were bunching, trying to control the wild rush of heat and nerves that danced inside of me.

S hadn't made any mistakes. Whoever he was, and whoever he thought *I* was, this... all of this was for me.

I'm Pet.

Snapping my eyes open, I stared at the glimmering cupcake. The 'S' on top looked bigger, heavier than before. *This means he knows me. Do I know him?*

Dammit. I really did have a secret admirer! But who? Who could it possibly be?

Warily, I peered side to side, expecting to find someone watching me. Even in this busy office, I was essentially ignored.

Caressing the card-stock, I folded it carefully. Next to me the trashcan sat, mouth wide and waiting. Throwing this all away—the letter, the cupcake—would take no effort. Who would know? Who would care?

My hand with the letter dipped low.

He would care.

I hesitated. The cupcake sat there, expectant.

Lifting the dainty, frosted dessert, I took a bite. Vanilla and sugar exploded on my tongue. It was better than any cupcake I'd ever had. Smooth, rich; I came close to rolling my eyes back in my skull.

With one last look at the trashcan, I squeezed the letter. It was proof that this game was being played with me.

With *me*.

How could I end it, when I'd only just realized I was actually a player?

****

Inside my locker was a single box. The sight of it ramped up my adrenaline. Had I really missed opening these things so much?

No. It was more than that.

For the first time, I knew this gift was *for me*. That gave the whole experience a new allure. My guilt was gone, the lead in my guts melting into butterflies. What I experienced now was genuine excitement.

Collecting the box, I drove home, trying not to break the speed limit.

It had been over a week since the last gift; the lingerie that I now regretted throwing in my trash. I consoled myself by saying I couldn't have known. This was an esoteric game, I'd never been involved in anything like it.

Casualties were bound to happen.

I had, however, kept the emerald earrings. They'd gone unnoticed in my car's cup-holder. I'd found them minutes ago when I'd set my coffee into the deep indentation, spilling some when it didn't settle right.

Crossing my living room, I dropped my coat and keys on the floor. I wasn't thinking about being tidy. Opening the package was an obsession, an itch that needed to be scratched.

Migrating into my kitchen, I scooted into a chair and placed the box on the round wooden table. Like most of my furniture, it served its purpose, but that was all I could ask of it.

Reaching down, I noticed my hands were quaking. *Easy, easy.* Laughing nervously, I made tight fists. When I peeled the tape away, my fingers still trembled.

The package split open, a heavy object tumbling onto the table. It was thick as a carrot, but shaped like some odd, swooping curve that tapered on one end, wide and blunt on the other.

Stroking the pliant, magenta surface, I blinked. "What the hell?" There was no one to answer my question. No one but S, perhaps.

Searching in the box, I found a note.

Pet,

This is a special, unique treat that I believe will bring you great pleasure.

Enjoy it to your heart's content. The idea of that will keep me very, very warm.

And very hard.

—S

Pursing my lips, I folded the paper and put it aside. Lifting the magenta-thing, I twisted it gently in my palms. The small nub on the top of one side was squishy; I prodded it, testing the weight of the device.

When I gave the base a firm squeeze, it came to life.

Gasping, I dropped the vibrating object. On top of my kitchen table it buzzed in place, the fat nub wiggling obscenely.

And then I knew.

I knew exactly what this was.

He'd sent me a damn dildo.

I grabbed the toy, struggling to turn it off. The base had a hidden switch, and after a few presses, the whole thing shut down.

My kitchen was eerily quiet without the constant buzzing.

Sweat caught in the pit of my collar bone. *He sent me something like THIS?* I'd seen sex toys, I wasn't a total prude. But I'd never owned any, and certainly had never been *gifted* any.

What did he expect me to do with this?

Flustered, I bit my lip. *Right. I know what he expects.* After all, he'd said the thought of it would get him *hard*.

It was such a perverse concept. My mind was vibrating harder than the toy had. *This is too much. He can't be serious.* How bold could one man be?

Leaning back in my chair, I eyed the toy like it was a snake. Touching it, I jerked my arm back instinctively. Then, breathing into my gut, I cradled it in my palm. The material it was made from was luxurious, not hard plastic.

Even here, S had extravagant taste.

Frowning, I studied the object again. Imagining my benefactor buying this with me in mind... it was another facet to this whole game.

I can't act too oblivious, I told myself. *Part of me had to know what this guy was after.*

But what was *I* after?

Accepting clothes and jewelry, building up a slow appreciation and knowledge about this stranger... that was safe. That was in my comfort zone. I suppose I thought, with time, I'd meet this S and it would be—

What? I cut my thoughts off brutally. *You thought he'd want to give you flowers and take you on a stroll?*

A man who played clever games and talked about sexy photos, lingerie, and... and sex toys... No. I was a fool to act naive.

Gripping the vibrator, I sighed. He was taking us to a new level. My stomach was tingling with the idea. Was I ready to go this far?

Standing, I carried the toy into my bedroom. Just the act of crossing the threshold had me shivering. *Did he really picture me using this on myself?*

I traded it to my other hand uneasily. *Did he imagine me moaning, writhing until I finally came from his gift?*

How much would that turn him on?

Blushing, I shoved the dildo into my bedside drawer. I didn't have the guts to trash it, not after thinking about the poor lingerie I'd lost.

I also wasn't ready to indulge in this side of things.

Not yet.

And maybe... never.

- Chapter Five -

Alexis

"You look different."

Flinching, I stared up at Laralie as she leaned over my desk. "What?" I asked.

She pointed to me, smiling slyly. "Your outfit, the way you walk... Oh my gosh, you're seeing someone, aren't you?"

Scrunching up my eyebrows, I sank low in my chair. "Shh! And no, I'm not. I'm just trying out some new stuff."

Her stare said she didn't believe me. How could I blame her?

In the past few days my clothing had shifted. S had sent me gorgeous shoes, brand name jeans, dresses with layers and even a Burberry coat.

It was only a matter of time before others noticed.

Rocking in my seat, I pretended my computer screen was very interesting. "It's seriously nothing, Laralie."

"It's clearly something."

"It's not!"

"It's—"

A phone call interrupted our banter. Wagging a finger at Laralie to quiet her down, I lifted the receiver. "Salvador and Goldheart, how can I help you?"

"Yes," a decidedly male voice said. "I'm looking for Alexis Willow."

My back went ramrod straight. Laralie saw, and she hovered close with a curious gleam in her eyes. "Uh, yes. This is Alexis speaking."

"Alexis, this is Detective Roose. Do you have a few minutes?"

A detective? My heart started to thump. "What's this about?"

I heard him shifting in his chair. "Miss Willow, I'm going over some old files. This may seem abrupt, but you're familiar with the bank robbery at Old Stone, right? Five years back or so?"

Old Stone.

I clutched the receiver, the edges of my vision going blurry. Had I heard him right? Yes, there was no doubt. But why... why now, and why ever...

"Ma'am? Are you there?"

My ears were burning with a hollow noise. Everything sounded so distant. Laralie was watching me. From her face, I knew I looked terrified.

Clearing my throat, I whispered, "Sorry, yes, I'm here."

"Did you hear my question?"

Twisting my chair, I half-faced away from Laralie. "Yeah. I remember Old Stone, why are you calling about that?"

The detective—had he said his name was Roose?—cleared his throat. "I'd rather talk about it in person. I just need a few minutes of your time. Can we meet up this Thursday?"

Images were rolling through my head. Things I really, truly did not want to think about.

Not now, and not ever.

I worked my tongue, forcing words. "What's there to say, it was five years ago. You probably know everything about it."

His chuckle was kind, but it did nothing for me. "I really don't want to do this over the phone. Let's just say, some new things have come to light. I can meet you at your office. It's Salvador and Goldheart, right?"

My jaw tightened. Of course he knew where I worked, he'd called in and found me. I wasn't shocked, but it left me sour. "I guess I don't need to give you the address, do I?"

He sounded like he was smiling. "I won't take up your day or change your schedule. It would really help me, ma'am. Really."

More than anything, I ached to tell him no. That robbery... how could it come back to haunt me? I'd forgotten to breathe, so when I did, it sounded desperate. "Alright. A few minutes on Thursday."

"Thank you." Unless I was mistaken, he was genuinely relieved. "Well, I'll let you go back to your business. See you in a week, Miss Willow." Then there was just dead air.

Turning, I set the phone down, fingers cramping.

"What was that about?" Laralie asked, bending over the top of my desk.

I stared at her, dazed. "A detective wants to talk to me."

She pushed her lips together, eyes becoming huge saucers. "You? What did *you do*, Alexis?"

"Nothing." Fixing my hair, I sighed. "I don't know. It's about..." Shit, even saying the name was a struggle. "You remember the bank robbery at Old Stone?"

Her face came to life, sparkling with interest. "I knew I heard you say that name! The robbery that wasn't much of a robbery? Of course I remember! What does that have to do with you?"

I had some idea. I didn't dare say it.

"I wonder," she mused out loud.

I cocked my head. "Go on."

"Well!" Splaying her fingers, she grinned in barely held back excitement. "Okay. Maybe this detective is looking for information on Old Stone because of the new bank hacking!"

I spluttered. "W—what?" Was the room suddenly very warm? "Who hacked another bank? How do you know this?"

Laralie crinkled her nose. "I don't know *who*. No one does. And they didn't even manage it, it was just an attempt that triggered the security system or something. It's been all over the news, how have you not heard about it?"

Truthfully, I'd been so busy with my own sordid, personal game with S, I hadn't turned my TV or radio on in ages.

I cupped the side of my skull. It was swelling, ready to split. A new hacking? A detective who wanted to meet me? This was all too much. Standing, I dusted myself off. "It's getting late, I'm going to head out."

"Aw, Alexis!" Pouting, Laralie crossed her arms. "Don't keep me in the dark. You're becoming very intriguing lately, you know?"

The smile that crossed my face was thin as ice. "I guess so."

I didn't want to be interesting.

****

My mailbox was empty.

Gawking, I continued to squint into the locker, like I'd manifest a package into existence if I stared long enough.

Why was there nothing? A single day hadn't gone by where I didn't receive a gift from S. Not since I'd started accepting the packages again, anyway.

The gaping slot taunted me.

Something is wrong. Snow flooded my veins, pricking my anxiety. Shutting the mailbox, I walked on numb legs back to my car. Surely this was just a weird mistake. Perhaps he was busy.

Yes, I admonished myself, climbing into my car. *Don't be greedy. It isn't like I should just expect these gifts all the time!*

I kept a structured life. His treats had become part of my routine.

Shaking myself, I tapped my cheeks. I had to get a grip. I was being silly.

Laughing at my overreaction, I left the post office. Tomorrow, things would surely go back to normal.

Except...

They didn't.

Day after day, as I ripped open my locker with more desperation, I found nothing inside. Sometimes bills, or junk, but no more packages.

S had vanished from my life.

It made no sense, and it had happened so suddenly. I felt like an addict, craving relief but never finding it. His game had wormed under my skin. I didn't know how to turn off my desire, or my depression.

What had I done to upset him?

That was the only conclusion. I *had* done something. Why else would he punish me?

Punish. I tasted the word, scowling. Was that really it? In what way could I have wronged this man I still hadn't met?

My week was bleak. One day faded into the next, and when Saturday came, I was swaying into gloom. It was pathetic, I knew that. But I swear, it felt exactly like...

Like a breakup.

S had broken up with me. *I guess I became boring.* The thought was wretched.

I went back and forth all day, resisting the urge to go to the post office. The clock ticked like it was stuffed with honey. Each hour dragged until I could think of nothing else.

I was weak.

And I didn't care.

The ride to the post office was quick. I'd delayed until the building was near closing time. Rushing, I pulled into the lot so hard my tires kicked up dirt.

I have to hurry. What if, what if today...

The slight hope that this time, a gift would be waiting for me, was enough to make me run. Shoving inside, I stared straight at my locker.

Facing away from me was a man.

It was that lanky, young guy who worked here, his jacket partially hiding his uniform. He'd opened my locker on top, where the workers could drop the mail inside.

In his hand... was a letter.

"It's you," I gasped, startling him.

Twisting around, that guy—Kerie— stared at me in disbelief. The letter in his hand crinkled from his tension. "Excuse me?"

Step by step, I approached him. Rage and confusion tormented my insides. Suddenly, everything was clicking together. "Of course. It's the only way you could put the packages in my locker without addressing them. You're..." I swallowed. "S?"

His brow knotted, but he didn't move. "No. You've got the wrong idea."

I stopped, my heels digging in. We were mere feet away. "Don't lie to me." After everything, my mystery admirer would dare try and—

"I'm serious!" Lifting his arms like I had a gun on him, he offered the letter. "The guy you're talking about? He's been paying me to stick this stuff in your mail. I don't know who he is, but I'm sorry for being so sly. Just please, don't tell my boss."

My confidence crumbled. Taking the envelope, I looked from it, to Kerie. No. There was definitely no way this young, nervous man was my S.

"You met him?" All at once, my ribs became too small. "What's he like?"

Crookedly smiling, Kerie shrugged. "I don't know. I can't judge guys. I guess he looks fine."

"No, not what he *looks* like, I meant..." It didn't matter. I could tell from Kerie's comment that he would give me nothing. Did I care what S looked like? Maybe somewhere deep down I did, but our connection was woven from something else. Not rock hard abs or chiseled cheekbones, this relationship was—how did I even describe it?

Fuller. Deeper.

Meaningful.

I squeezed the letter, then brushed it softly. "So what, this guy just showed up one day and demanded you put things in my mail?"

"Kind of. He came in, told me he needed me to slip those packages to you. I tried to explain it was against the rules, but he offered me a *lot* of money." His blush was furious. "Really, I'm sorry for playing dumb."

It was hard to stay angry. Especially now, with news from S between my fingers. I clutched the letter tightly. "I won't tell anyone. But, if I'm ever in here when he is… promise you'll point him out to me."

Kerie shifted side to side, hands in his pockets. "If I can be subtle, okay. I will."

That was good enough.

I started to turn, cradling the square of paper like it was made of glass. Kerie called out to me, stopping my retreat. "Wait!" I turned back. "There's one more thing in here." Reaching through the top of the locker, he withdrew a slim, long box, about the size of a pillow.

There was another gift, and I'd almost left it behind.

"Thanks," I whispered, taking it gently. My face hurt; when had I begun smiling? "I—I should go. Good night, Kerie."

He gave me a brief wave, leaning on the locker until I was long out of sight.

I wondered what he thought about all of this. For almost a month, he'd been accepting money in exchange for playing the part of a stealthy delivery boy. S was determined to keep his identity secret from me.

My curiosity burned brighter than ever.

Clicking off the car engine, I gathered everything and entered my house. Again, I did a quick check, rushing to make sure no one was hiding inside. I almost skipped it, but old habits die hard.

Making myself a cup of tea, I sat on the couch, looking between the two objects. Which should I open first, the letter or the box? They'd each give their own brand of answers.

In the end, I was too eager for the intimacy that his written words gave me.

Setting my mug down, I pried the envelope open carefully. Already, heat was swirling in my core, my heart punching against my ribs. This man had me wrapped around his little finger.

The intoxication of a new message made me not even care.

Pet,

I'm sorry for making you wait. I wanted to give you a taste of what it would be like to live without me. For some time now, you've been accepting my gifts.

Now it's my turn.

I want my gift.

I want you.

Our game is ready for the next level— something far more personal.

Something... intimate.

Tomorrow night, I'll send someone to pick you up. Go with them. No questions, no backing out. I don't want this to end here, and I suspect you don't either.

Enjoy the dress. I'm eager to see you in it.

P.S. Wear the earrings.

—S

Opening the box, I unfolded the glossy, brilliantly silver gown. It had a lovely weight to it, split up one side and with a back that dipped daringly low. It was more beautiful than anything else I owned.

Bending close, I caught of whiff of something. It wasn't the feminine perfume of a woman. This was a vague, but tantalizing scent of the mountains. It reminded me of a winding trail that weaved beneath ancient oak trees. As I inhaled again, goosebumps rippled over my flesh.

Is that what he smells like?

It was easy to imagine S packaging this dress up. His hands would be deft, folding the cloth as he took great care with the present meant only for me.

For me.

He'd called me his gift to him. *He wants me to meet him tomorrow night?* Lifting the letter, I read it again and again. *Finally face to face.* I'd get to lay eyes on the man who'd been seducing me from afar.

Once, I would have debated longer. I'd have sat up and paced, trying to weigh the danger against the benefit of agreeing to see a stranger. I didn't know S, I only felt like I did. He could be anyone, or anything.

I know what he is.

Sensual.

Wicked.

Dominant.

It was the most unlikely thing for me to hug that dress, and know in my heart what I'd decided. Against all odds, this man had changed me in such a short time.

After weeks of letters and gifts, of playing this elusive game...

I was finally going to meet S.

- Chapter Six -
Alexis

The squeak of tires outside turned my anxiety up another notch. Cracking the blinds, I peered at what was waiting for me.

The limo sat like a great panther, crouched in the shadows out on the street. One bite, and it would swallow me whole. The idea made me nauseous.

I'd felt so sure about my decision to commit to this meeting, but faced with the moment... I was fraying on my edges.

All I had to do was not open my door, not cross the sidewalk, and not climb into that limousine. If I sat right here in my unfairly magnificent dress and did nothing, everything would end. I was sure he'd refuse to give me another chance.

I'd be free.

It was so simple. But...

I want to know who he is. That information was being dangled in front of me. After weeks of surprises and alluring letters, how could I possibly cut off contact now?

Standing, I straightened my outfit and walked stiffly outside. When I appeared, the driver-side door of the vehicle opened. S had said he'd send someone, but I still froze, paranoid this stranger could actually be him.

The man wore dark, starched clothing. Silver buttons cascaded down the front of his jacket. He was older, weathered and sporting a thick white beard. He tipped his hat to me. "Evening. I'm Jessop, ma'am. Mister S sent me to pick you up."

In my gut, I knew Jessop was exactly what he appeared to be—a chauffeur. That didn't smooth the wrinkles in my veins. Rocking in place, I clutched my purse.

"Please," he said, opening the door for me. "Climb inside. It's very cozy."

He isn't dangerous, I told myself firmly. I had no way to know that, I was just trusting my gut to keep me safe. Inching forward, I tried to match his easy smile. "Thanks. You can call me Alexis."

"As you wish." He had friendly, but perceptive, eyes. I bet he could tell how anxious I was.

Hell, anyone could.

Once I was inside the limo, I sank into the soft cushions. Around me, everything was lit up by tiny, fairy-like lights. An open bottle of wine was waiting for me. S was a smart man; in this situation, who *wouldn't* need a drink?

Like he'd heard my thoughts, Jessop said, "Help yourself to anything you see."

My fingers brushed the neck of the bottle. The name on the label was foreign to me. *I'm sure it costs a fortune. But he left it here so I could have it.*

It was a blessing, I needed some liquid courage.

Pouring the rich, ruby liquid into a glass, I looked towards the front of the limo. Jessop still had the divider lowered.

"Comfortable?" he asked.

Motioning around, I said, "Definitely. It's really nice in here."

He nodded in approval, guiding the limo down the street. I wanted to drill him for info, except I couldn't think of a subtle way to do it. Instead, I sipped the wine, the tart, fruity flavor spreading over my tongue like a warm sunrise.

Settling deeper in my seat, I crossed my legs and tried to enjoy the silence. Through it all, I kept swinging my foot over my knee. Every few minutes, I'd adjust on the seat, fidgeting beyond control.

Time melted into a meaningless lump. I didn't have a clue how long we'd been driving for, or where we were even headed. I'd finished the glass of wine, and was on a second, when the limo slowed down. "We're here," Jessop said, cracking the divider.

Squinting through the tinted glass, I saw he'd parked in front of a reddish glowing entrance. There were men outside, arms crossed to show off their muscles. *Security guards,* I realized. *What is this place? A club?*

Jessop opened my door, letting the cool night air waft into the car. His gloved hand waited, body language making it obvious he expected me to step out. He wasn't being presumptuous; what else was I going to do after coming so far?

Taking his hand, I put my shaking, heeled shoe onto the curb. The men by the door looked my way. Leaning towards Jessop, I whispered, "He's inside?" The driver gave a quick nod. "Where are we, exactly?" I could see no name on the brick building.

"The Red and Ripe, one of his favorite places." Nodding towards the doors, he ducked his head. "Go on inside, he's waiting for you."

Waiting for me.

I hovered there, poised on that dark street that was crowded by old brick buildings and empty warehouses. I didn't know the area, but it had to be a shadier part of downtown. Was this really where I was supposed to meet S?

Did you expect the Four Seasons? I mused to my own chagrin. *Who cares where I am?* Truthfully, I'd have met him at a greasy diner and been just as excited.

Jessop waited, the guards waited, and I stood sandwiched between their stares. Clearing my throat, I strolled over the cracked ground towards the burly men. Their chins lifted, eyes looking me over more hungrily than I liked.

I wasn't used to being ogled, and my arms crossed over the creamy skin of my chest that the dress had left exposed. "Hey there," I said, my words a white puff in the cold air. "Mind if I go on inside?"

They exchanged a quick look. "What's your name, honey?" one of them asked.

My lips crinkled in a frown. "Alexis, it's Alexis. Not honey."

He snorted, glancing at a list in his hand. The other guard said nothing, but he kept leering. "Fine, Alexis. You're not on here."

"What?" I dropped my hands. "That's impossible."

They both rolled their eyes, like they heard this a lot. "No Alexis on here, doll. Get in your fancy car and—"

"Pet," I said quickly, my mouth faster than my brain. *That's what he'd put down.* "Check under Pet."

Running a fat finger down the chart, the balder of the two guys nodded. "In that case, looks like you can go in." Standing aside, he gestured to the dark door set into the building. "Have a *fun* time."

Behind me, I heard tires rumbling; Jessop was pulling the limo out of view. If I wanted to back out now, I'd have a hell of a time.

Standing taller, I stepped past the men with my jaw set in a line. Pushing through a thick and heavy red curtain, I was assaulted by the thrum of music. In its wake came the heat of bodies.

People filled the space, the room rounded to match the curved ceiling. Drapery hung from dark wooden beams, and the lights along the walls kept up the constant crimson hue. The air was all cinnamon, making my skin tingle like I'd been rolling in gingerbread.

The Red and Ripe looked *nothing* like the outside of the building.

Stunned, I made myself move deeper. Around me, the customers talked or danced. I'd snuck into a few clubs when I was younger. The danger of getting caught had been thrilling. I was reminded of that feeling now.

My buzz from the wine had evaporated. Smoothing my dress, I started to hurry towards the bar in the corner. I was burning with a need to stay busy, because standing still meant waiting.

Fingers gripped my wrist, stopping me in my tracks. I wasn't ready to be touched, and on impulse, I started to yank away. "Excuse me!" I gasped, spinning to face my assailant. "Just who do you think..."

And like that, my words vanished to mix with the music.

The man who towered over me didn't move. Somehow, still, he had this air around him that spoke of being fluid—being fast. His hand grazed down mine, touching my fingertips and creating a burst of static.

His eyes slid over me, coating my soul as they searched. They moved as patiently as honey down a spoon, shining the same shade. The red hue of the club lights turned his cropped, dark hair glossy.

He'd chosen to wear a coal-colored shirt that bared his forearms. The tendons rippled, making the intricate tattoos slither and writhe obscenely. His jeans were a rich onyx, the jacket draped over one shoulder just as dark.

The edge of his smile spoke to me. A private secret, a little smirk that said *I know what you want from me.*

I'd never been so exposed in my life.

Arching an eyebrow, he darted a hand forward. Before I could react, he stroked my earring. "I was right. They're beautiful on you."

Fireworks went off in my brain. I knew the truth. There was no doubt.

This was S.

Blood flooded every pore. I was tingling where he'd touched me, even after his hand fell to his side. This was really happening. The man that had been courting me secretly, tempting me with all sorts of intriguing gifts, was just inches away.

I forgot how to form words—even sounds.

"Did I break that pretty mouth of yours?" he asked.

Flustered, I swallowed to wet my throat. I had so much I wanted to say. So many questions. Looking him in the eye, I whispered over the music, "It's really you."

He threw his head back, laughing earnestly. When he finally looked down at me again, there was an extra layer of depth in his vibrant stare. "Yes, it's really me."

"I didn't know what to expect," I admitted, smiling shyly. "Every time I read your letters, I tried to imagine your face, or how you'd sound in person. I even thought you might be someone I knew, instead of a stranger."

The dimple of his smile moved upwards. "Stranger." He tasted the word. "Since you didn't know what I looked like, what gave *me* away, Pet?"

Pet. That fucking word. It was dripping with erotic, taboo promises. My shiver was full-bodied, it shook my toes in my high-heels. I didn't think people actually swooned in real life, but here I was, ready to collapse towards the floor.

Shifting my weight, I adjusted my dress. "Who else would bring up my earrings like you did?"

He glanced at them again, bending a hair closer to me. I could smell that familiar crisp, mountain scent. "You're right, I'm sure most people would be distracted by *other* parts of you first."

The spark originated in my chest continued between my thighs. I clenched my knees, the pressure too delicious.

Peering off to the side, he saw something I didn't. "Come on. It's too crowded out here." He took my elbow, his other hand grazing on the small of my back. It was an intimate touch for someone I'd just met. It should have felt wrong.

With him, it felt beyond right.

While there was an air of mystery surrounding him, he radiated protectiveness. Enough that I let him guide me through the throngs of dancers until we pulled up beside a curtained wall.

A man was waiting there, his body bulging like it wanted to escape his black jeans and white button-down. He took one look at us, then wordlessly spread the curtain. S smiled, leading me into a tiny alcove.

The space was just big enough for us and a table, everything glowing like the inside of a lit pumpkin. We were alone, the rest of the club washed away. How thick were the walls that they could mute so much of the noise?

"Sit," he said, gesturing as he released me.

I missed his touch, wishing he'd just kept hold. *Get some self control!* Settling into the chair, he soon copied me, sitting on the opposite side.

Weaving his fingers together, he set them on the hard surface of the table. The playful light in his eyes highlighted the beautiful angles of his jaw. I cared more about the substance of this man than what he might have looked like, but... I couldn't deny it.

I was ecstatic—and amazed—by how handsome he was.

The very air around him felt like it was *breeding* sex. If people could bottle his essence, they'd make a fortune.

"Do I make you nervous?"

His bluntness threw me off. "The situation makes me a little uneasy. I mean, I'm here because you've been sending me all these letters and gifts. People don't meet like this."

His head bent towards one side. "I meant, do *I* make you nervous, Pet."

A flutter rolled through me. I rocked in my chair, hands balling in my lap. *But he must know my real name, if he had cupcakes sent to my work.* How much *did* he know about me, and how?

That led me to a new question, one that had been growing for some time. "What does the 'S' stand for?" I blurted, unable to hold back.

Running a finger over his cheek, he gestured at my dress. "Take a guess. I've been leaving hints for you."

Blinking, I stroked the hem of my outfit. *What does he mean?* It was smooth, and it fit me wonderfully. Just wearing it was enough to get my heart going.

Hints... What was the clue? He'd sent me so many things.

Tilting my head, I tugged at my hair out of habit. In the process, I flicked the edge of my earring. In the crimson lights, my dress looked more maroon than silver, just like my earrings would. It didn't matter. I knew what he was trying to tell me.

"Silver," I breathed out, smacking my palms onto the tabletop in delight. Looking up, I found him watching me with hunger in his amber eyes. "It's Silver, isn't it?"

Winking, he slid his palms over the table until he scooped my fingers up. He moved fast

—trapping me. "I love how fucking clever you are. Yes, Silver. And you look *gorgeous* wearing my name."

Blushing along my throat, I rubbed my knees together. From the start, he'd been branding me. I hadn't even noticed.

S had left his mark where the world could see.

I didn't know how to feel about that. It was bold, and kind of crazy, too. He was letting everyone know I was claimed.

That I belonged to him.

I became conscious of how ridiculous this was; a man sending me secret gifts and courting me from afar. Shivering, I pulled at my hands, but he just held tighter. Licking my lower lip, I met his intense eyes. "Silver can't be your real name."

Those eyes hardened like ancient glaciers. "To you, it is."

I controlled the tightening that slid between my ribs. His answer hurt, but clearly he wanted to keep his identity a secret. He must have a good reason for that. "Alright, so what should I call you? S, or Silver?"

"Which do you prefer?"

His hands were warm on mine, holding me down as easily as if he'd been clutching my jugular. But honestly, it was his stare that kept me planted where I was. Or, almost planted.

I *was* shifting side to side with nervous energy.

"I like Silver," I said, blushing as I admitted it.

He showed me his row of straight teeth. "Good. I happen to love hearing my name from your lips, almost as much as I love calling you Pet."

That made my pussy twitch. I crossed my ankles, I'd already crossed my thighs as tight as I could. Was it weird to feel so aroused by this man? *I'm probably desperate from years of no action.* That didn't sound right. So what had driven me here?

"You look uncomfortable," he said softly, sliding his fingers from mine.

Closing my hands, I pulled them to my chest. They felt empty. "I am. I mean, how can I *not* be? I have so many questions about you—about all of this."

"Then ask away."

My jaw slid open. "What?"

"Ask away." He rolled his palm down his chest, taking my attention with it. "If you have questions, let me hear them."

I didn't hesitate. "Why *me?*"

Grinning ear to ear, Silver looked me over. The twinkle in his eye had a million shards, a million ways to leave me guessing at his thoughts. "That's a very good question. And one I'm not ready to answer."

I scowled. "That's not fair."

"No?" he asked, chuckling.

"You said I could ask questions, but you dodged the first one."

"I said you could ask. I never said I'd answer."

"So you *won't* tell me anything?"

"Try again, let's see."

Drumming my fingers on my hips, I glanced side to side. "This club, Jessop said it was one of your favorites. Do you own it? Is that how you..." *Make your money.* I bit my tongue. I didn't want to sound like I cared about money; I didn't. But I was curious, and I couldn't deny wondering how he'd paid for everything he'd sent me, including a hired limo.

"The Red and Ripe doesn't belong to me." Smiling, he eyed the room we sat in. "But it's a very interesting place."

Interesting? No, you're what's interesting.

Something nudged me under the table. I realized what it had to be.

His shoe.

He glided the shiny tip along my bare ankle. When I glanced back up, ready to let fly another question or two, I simply froze.

Silver was watching me, yet all the humor was gone. His tight lips said he was holding something back, and the heat in his eyes screamed lust. Raw, honest lust.

I said, "Um, so, if you don't own this club, then..."

"You said you hadn't been here before, right?" He didn't let me answer, he pushed his chair back and stood. "Let me show you around. You can see what I like so much about it."

Every question I have, he keeps dodging. I still knew nothing about this man. I was ready to feel furious. Amazingly, I obeyed him and stood. More amazingly, when he reached out to place his palm on my shoulder, I let him.

There was a moment where I trembled, languishing in the electric jolt that arose from our contact. I think he must have felt it, too, because he glanced down at me and hesitated.

We hovered there, the only sound between us was our own breathing. In the red glow, his eyes absorbed all light. They became black, richly dark like a fine coffee. I could drown in those eyes.

He flared his nostrils, filling his broad chest. On my shoulder, his fingers dug in. The fierceness turned my lower belly into whipped cream.

"You're dangerous," he whispered.

"Me?" I smiled dubiously. "How am I—"

"Trust me, Pet. The things you're making me resist doing to you right now..." He breathed out. "I didn't think holding back would be so hard."

My cheeks bloomed, my heart ticking in a circle. This man wasn't scared to tell me that he wanted me.

Breaking eye contact, he pushed me gently through the curtain. Instantly the thrum of music hit; I'd forgotten the rest of the world existed. His presence was constant, beating out the cloying sweat and drumbeat of the other club-goers.

Easily, he forced us through the bodies. I tried to pay attention, but my senses were working against me. My nerves itched to focus on *him*. His palm on my shoulder, his rough breathing by my ear... Silver was exactly what I thought he'd be.

The fraying rope that kept me from gripping his shoulders and begging him to put out the damn ache he'd been creating in me for weeks was near snapping. This was nothing like me—I didn't spend my time thinking about sex!

And now it's all I can think about with him.

"There," he hushed, stopping us on the outskirts of the room. "Look."

Following his lead, I stared across at the walls. I noticed the indents—much like the one we'd been inside, except there were no curtains on these.

In one of the concave rooms, I saw shapes writhing. My brain was slow, or I was denying what I was seeing. Either way, it didn't click immediately that these were people. Sweat glinted off of naked skin, the couple wrapped up in their own world.

They didn't care who watched.

The man was on his back, the woman riding him fiercer than a bull in a rodeo. Her breasts were being mauled in his palms, skin redder than the lights could have made them.

I... what...

Not once did either of them look at the crowd. She arched her spine, gripping his shoulders and moaning in sinful delight. In each of the rooms, a couple—or more—was doing the same thing.

They were all wantonly fucking in public.

Clutching at my dress, I pushed the wave of emotions down. Was this fear in my guts, or was I getting turned on?

A hand brushed my wrist. "Are you alright?" Silver asked in my ear. "You're breathing heavily."

"Fine. I'm fine." Stepping back, I bumped into him; I'd forgotten how close we were.

Tucking his arm around my waist, he pressed his palm against my forehead. I could see the tiny crease in the middle of his bottom lip. "You're burning the fuck up."

Of course I am, I thought sluggishly. *I'm watching a bunch of strangers screwing in a corner.* I could still hear them panting.

"Are you getting excited?" he asked me, his words burrowing into my ear. "Are you imaging doing that, fucking where everyone can watch you shake and shiver and come?"

My legs became noodles. He was being too crass, my mind resisting as my pussy threatened to ruin my panties. His form leaned into me, and I swore I felt the growing shape of his hard-on.

This was too much.

What the hell was I doing in this place?

From the corner of my eye, I spotted the neon-cherry exit sign. "I need to get some air," I stammered. If I stayed, I didn't know what would happen. Did he want us to do *that?* Just go wild where everyone could see? Was he an exhibitionist, a voyeur, something else?

"Air? Of course, I'll walk with you—"

"Sorry, I can't—I'm sorry." Unable to explain how the surging desire was overwhelming me, I pushed away from him. His fingers drifted down my arm, threatening to snatch me back before I could run.

Then we were apart, and I was stumbling for the door.

Shoving around the crowd, I rushed out into the cool night. Gasping, I threw my head back. Around me, the pulse of music and bodies faded, the heavy door clanking shut.

Why am I here?

The question swam up abruptly. I couldn't bury it. This place was a perverted sex club—Silver had taken me to an actual *sex club!*

A month ago, if I'd been asked to predict my future, I would never have guessed this was coming. None of it. Fuck, a million guesses and I'd still have been wrong.

Me, Alexis Willow—notoriously quiet and lame—meeting up with some smartly-dressed, power-oozing man who kept calling me Pet? Gifts were one thing, this escalation went beyond my limits.

I'm an idiot, I reprimanded myself. Pushing my hand to my forehead, I swiped my hair back and laughed. "What's wrong with me?" I asked the night sky. The scent of garbage was rank in my nose, but I breathed deeper, filling my lungs with it. "Did I think I could really mesh with a guy like him?"

Years ago, I would have fit in better... but... No. That was a pointless thought. I wasn't the same girl. My life was different, *I* was different.

Ever since that single day.

The grip that came down on my arm yanked me from my pitiful thoughts. It was firm, steel and iron.

105

Silver, I thought on reflex. *He came outside to find me.*

But something was wrong. Why hadn't I heard the door open? In fact, it should have hit me, I was still right up on it.

Fear snaked into my heart. In my ear, the breathing of the other person was raspy and labored. That was when I knew. Even before I turned, looking into those yellow and red-veined eyes, I knew.

The hand on my shoulder didn't belong to Silver.

- Chapter Seven -

Alexis

He spun me around, clutching for my wrists. It was an older man, his face hard, his smile too soft. Inside his eyes, hard-packed black ash focused on me.

"Hey there," he purred. "You looked lonely out here. Thought I'd say hi."

It's happening again.

"Let go of me!" Wrenching my shoulder, I worked to get free, but he only squeezed harder.

Chuckling, he spun me from the wall, forcing me down the empty alley. Trash slid under my heels, and I regretted wearing them. In sneakers, I could have run faster—fought back harder.

I'm not going to give up!

Gritting my teeth, I swung my body backwards. "Help!" I screamed, echoing off the wet bricks. "Someone please, help me! *Help me!*"

Scowling, my attacker rounded on me, strangling my wrists. My skin was numb; I didn't care. "Shut up!" he snarled, pushing me against the rough alley wall. The hard texture was cool under my exposed spine. "You make another sound and I'll smash that pretty mouth right in!"

Breathing through clenched teeth, I leveled my glare on his. *Fight!* I begged my body. On impulse, I jammed my head forward, hoping I'd crush his nose with my skull. He managed to lean away, but the surprise in his wide eyes gave me strength. "*Let me go!*" I shouted, throat going hoarse.

The world needed to hear me. Surely someone would realize I was in danger. Did no one care?

Curling his lips back, almost feral, my attacker laughed. "You fucking bitch, you tried to break my nose! You think that's funny? *Huh?*" He shook me violently. Everything in my skull banged together, mushing into paste.

No one is coming.

The cold realization was sobering.

If I don't fight back, I'm dead.

I'm gone.

But I was too dazed, my feet couldn't get a grip on the slimy earth. It didn't matter how much I ached to hurt this man, he was winning.

Abruptly my attacker released me, stumbling to the side like he'd been hit by a car.

"What the fuck do you think you're doing to her?"

Silver had a voice hotter than the lava swirling in the Earth's core. The same vibrant anger reflected in his glare.

Lifting my head, I gawked at him. Had he heard my cries through the brick walls and come searching for me? "Help," I croaked, slumping to my knees.

He spared me a look, but his attention was laser focused on the other man.

My attacker was rubbing his jaw, blood staining his teeth. Wild-eyed, he glanced between us both. Rabid dogs don't use logic, and this man was close to foaming at the mouth. "You want that girly for yourself, that it, big man?"

Silver laughed, the sound echoing through the alley. He might as well have blown a trumpet, it would have shocked us both just as much. "Do I *want* her? She's already mine."

That admission sang into my ears and remained. I didn't try to deny his claim, that was how firmly it clung to my heart. *Getting attacked must have shook something loose in my brain.* That had to be it.

Spitting on the ground, the wretched man eyeballed Silver, then me. Spreading his fingers, he threw up his hands. I tensed, expecting him to launch forward and attack again. "Whatever, fuck you both! I'm gone."

Just like that, the man who had tried to drag me off became a coward. He slunk away, a shadow that faded into nothing around the alley's bend. If it weren't for the marks on my arms where he'd gripped me, I could have been waking from a nightmare.

"Are you alright?" Silver asked, taking my face in his palms.

Alright?

Was I *alright?*

It took me a moment, but I narrowed in on his amber eyes, his thick lashes, the gentle curve of his lips. "Yes," I whispered. The pain in my wrists faded into a dull throb. Mentioning it was pointless. "I'm fine, really."

He saved me.

Silver smiled, his skin warm and welcome on my cheeks. Never had I been held so tenderly, and never by a stranger.

Was someone who I had grown to know over the past month, even if through letters only, *really* a stranger? He'd made me gasp, made me burn, made me ache and long to finally be in his presence.

And now I was.

Every doubt that had chased me out of the club and into the cold alley became a wisp of meaningless smoke. In the flickering light of the single bulb above the club's backdoor, his skin danced—white to tan and back again. The syrup in his half-cocked grin lured me closer by the second.

I never meant to kiss him.

Magnetic explosions slid between us, my lashes fluttering with the raw energy. This man had rescued me, and call me a cliche, but what was more intoxicating than that?

When I pressed my mouth to his, we locked together. His hands curled around, capturing my hair and using it to get a grip. I still had the brick wall at my back, so with him in front of me, I was pinned. He crushed me further, the pressure of his body along my torso bringing out a low gasp.

"Fuck," he hissed, gliding his tongue along my upper lip. Whistles went off in my brain. "You taste so damn good, Pet. I want more... no, I *need* more."

Before I could reply, he kissed me again, making my lungs strain as the last of my air became stale. I needed to breathe, but the rest of me was too busy flourishing in the touch of a man who was pure sex and lust.

His knee slid between mine, forcing them apart. Warning sparks went off at the base of my skull, but I ignored them. The way he ground his leg along my panties was delicious.

Silver was all mouth, nibbling along my throat, my ear, everything. I was purring, lost in a range of desires. Fire clawed at my belly, dipping down until my pussy was melting.

This is happening, I thought in my haze. *This is really...*

Fingers brushed the front of my dress, nuzzling the hard shape of one nipple. The bolt of sexual need he lifted inside of me was stunning. It hit so hard that it shook away some of my sluggish lust.

We were standing in a filthy alley.

An alley outside of a sex club.

"Wait," I stammered, my hands pushing at his chest. "Not like this, I can't." The way my control had vanished from my body was terrifying. I was scared I wouldn't have enough left for even a hint of push-back from him.

"Alright," he breathed out tensely. "We can stop."

I froze. "What?"

His grin went wide. "It's fine. Did you think I was going to force you?" Chuckling, he leaned away and straightened out his jacket. How did he have all of his composure back when seconds ago he'd been growling in my ear?

Warily, I tilted my head and side-eyed him. I'd expected him to be mad, or to fight harder. His response threw me off balance. "You're really okay with us stopping?"

"Of course. But I won't lie..." Reaching down, he rubbed his palm over his massive erection, adjusting himself with a wince. "I'm hard as hell, I'd love to bend you over and finally bury myself deep between your thighs." My whole body went hot and red. "But if you want to stop, we'll stop. A lot has happened tonight. Taking you home might be best."

I opened my mouth, then shut it. "Alright. Yeah." *Taking me home. I can't predict this guy at all.*

115

Nodding, he dug for his keys. "Walk with me. I parked close by."

He doesn't want to leave me alone. I was grateful. I didn't want a repeat of earlier. "Should you let Jessop know he doesn't need to pick me up?"

Waving me to his side, Silver led us to the main street. "He knows not to come back unless I call for him. I don't use him very often, he has other clients keeping him busy. I assume there's no issue letting me be your chauffeur?"

"It's not a problem." A gust of air buffered me. Hugging myself, I tried to bite back a shiver.

Wordlessly, he slid his jacket from his shoulders. His exposed arms flexed, the dark red and rich black ink on his skin drawing my attention. In a second he'd placed the heavy, soft jacket around me. I breathed in to my limit, nuzzling my nose on the edge of the fabric.

Strolling through the night like this, we looked like a normal pair out on a date. I embraced that image, enjoying how our feet clicked in unison along the pavement.

As he'd said, the walk was short. The parking garage we entered was large, eternally quiet. When he slowed in front of a bright silver Mustang, I bit back a squeak.

Luxurious, cool, and silver. It could be his spirit animal.

He reached over, tugging the passenger side open for me. "Thanks," I said, ducking inside. The seats were warm, like they lived in a different world than the chilly evening.

"Comfortable?" he asked, clicking his seat belt in.

"Very. Your car is really cool." The second I said it, I started to blush.

Grinning, he let the engine rumble, turning us out of the garage. "I'm glad you like it."

We rode in silence, my bare knees crossing again and again. I couldn't get comfortable—I didn't know how to act. Only minutes ago, I'd kissed this man. *Kissed him,* after meeting him in person for the first time.

Watching my toes, I thought about the shoes I had on, how he knew my size. How he knew... far too much about me and my daily life.

And he doesn't want to tell me how.

Unable to hold back, I whispered into the quietness. "Are you a stalker?"

I knew it was a risk to ask him that if I was hoping to not ruin this evening any further. But I wasn't stupid, this man was playing a game with me, and as hot... as incredibly tempting as he was... I could end up hurt.

Stalkers were no joke.

They could be deadly.

He didn't glance at me, but I felt him shift. "What do you think?"

"I don't know what to think. You refuse to tell me anything about who you are, or why you contacted me at all." *Why me?* The eternal question.

Guiding his car down my street, he sighed. "You're too curious about things that don't matter."

"Of course they matter!"

He startled, staring at me and making me cover my mouth. Had I shouted? "All that matters is the end result."

Stiffening, I asked, "And what's that?"

"You." The engine died; he parked outside my house, his lights illuminating a raccoon as it fled my trash. "You're the end result. That's all I care about, Pet. The rest is just history."

The centers of his eyes widened. Before I could move, he clutched the nape of my neck and pulled me close. Our lips met, sealing together so he could race his tongue across mine. The kiss left me hazy, and then it was over.

"I want to see you again," he said flatly. "Tonight wasn't enough."

I was breathing heavy, unable to blink. "I—okay."

He pulled out a smartphone, then held out his palm to me. I knew what he wanted, so I fumbled my phone out and handed it to him. As I watched, he typed his number into mine, then vice versa.

Warily, I took my phone back. It was warm from his touch. "So... then..."

"I'll contact you soon. Get some sleep, okay?"

"Er, right. I—right." I was saying 'right' a lot. I was also having trouble making sense of this insane night.

Sliding off his jacket, I held it out. He lifted his eyebrows. "Keep it," he said firmly.

"No. It's fine, my house is right here." I couldn't take anything else from this man. Before he argued again, I dropped it on the seat and jumped out. When I got to my door, I twisted so I could look back at him.

Silver was watching me through his window, the sharp shadows making his expression impossible to read. But it didn't matter—not now. My insides had decided how to feel already. I was ruled by the memory of his kiss, of my own swollen lips and the slickness of his tongue.

He didn't drive away until I unlocked my door.

I stumbled inside, slamming it behind me. The calmness of my home just heightened the throbbing beat of my heart.

Holy shit.

Everything inside of me was buzzing. I'd fought down the urge to push further and see what Silver would do to me. Now, I was paying for it. *Female blue balls are real.* I laughed bitterly, running my fingers through my hair.

Kicking off my heels, I winced at the slight pain in my forearm. The attacker in the alley had left a bruise.

It could have been much worse.

Without Silver coming to my rescue, the night could have ended with much less of a fuzzy feeling. *But he did save me,* I reminded myself. Cradling my wrist, I remembered how intense Silver had looked when he'd stepped in.

Never *ever* had a man tried to protect me like that.

Clutching my dress hem, I did a tiny twirl. I was giddy, floating on my tired toes as I swayed around my home. The bubbles in my stomach were like carbonation and caffeine. I felt *alive.*

When had I last felt like this?

But I still have so many questions. Silver knew things about me that he shouldn't, not for someone I'd never met. He also enjoyed playing coy.

The reminder of his wicked smirks and hot lips set the other unsatisfied part of me into a frenzy. If he'd pushed me further in the alley, I'd have probably given in. Or maybe not. Fuck, I didn't know.

All I was sure of was that I was here, he was not, and I was decidedly turned on.

Slipping the dress off, I hung it in my closet and flopped nearly-naked onto my mattress. The blanket was cool on my boiling skin. For a long while, I did nothing but lie there with my face in the pillows.

I counted the seconds.

I tried to make my mind focus on boring things.

Finally, I flipped over and puffed at the hair in my face. *Dammit. I can't relax at all.* Twisting on my bed, I stared at the small table beside me. *Maybe... maybe I could...*

Swallowing, I reached out, opening the drawer. Inside, the purple sex toy waited for me. I'd stored it there, not wanting to throw it away but too embarrassed to actually use it.

What would I ever need it for?

Now, I knew.

- Chapter Eight -

Alexis

"You have some explaining to do," Laralie said, dropping a box onto my desk.

I jumped in my seat, yanked from my pleasant—if dirty—day dream. In it, Silver had come into my home, finding me enjoying the dildo he'd sent. In my head, he was happy to join in and teach me how to really use it.

I blinked down at the long box. "What's this?" I don't know why I asked. One look at the package, and it was obvious; Silver had sent me something.

Propping her elbows on the desk, Laralie leaned closer to me. She arched one fine eyebrow. "A delivery guy just showed up with this for you. Spill it, who is he?"

"Who is who?"

"The guy who's sending you surprise packages in the middle of the day!"

Grabbing the box, I pulled it closer. "Why do you think there's a guy at all?"

She rolled her eyes. "I'm not stupid, Alexis. I *know* you've been seeing someone. Look at how you carry yourself, it's obvious."

I tried to evaluate my own behavior. Had I been acting different? *Of course I have. My life is changing, Silver isn't like anyone I've dated before.*

Shit. Were we even dating? I had no clue what to call our situation.

Laralie cleared her throat. "Well?"

Running my hands over my face, I sighed. "Alright, okay. I'm seeing someone."

Gasping dramatically, she covered her mouth. I could still see the edges of her huge grin. "I knew it! What's he like? What did he send you?"

My eyes wandered to the box. "I don't know. He likes to shock me."

"Ooh, sounds fun!"

"Sort of." Grabbing my phone, I typed quickly: *How do you know where I work?* Sending the text, I peeked up at Laralie. She was bent halfway over my desk, reminding me of an excited puppy. "You don't expect me to open this in front of you, do you?"

"Oh yes, I do!"

In my hand the phone buzzed. With a flicker of excitement in my pulse, I read the message.

Silver: I know more about you than you realize.

The cryptic words made me freeze.

"Alexis? You okay?"

"Yeah." I buried the phone in my pocket. "I'm fine, don't worry." *What the hell does he mean?* "You really won't let me open this up alone?"

Her teeth glinted. "I'll stalk you into the bathroom if I have to."

I hope it isn't more sex toys. Peering side to side, I nodded. "Okay, but keep this between us." Gripping the ribbon, I slid it free. Then, I eased the lid off of the box.

Together, we both inhaled sharply.

The dress was like a waterfall of mercury. I lifted it high enough for us both to see the low-cut back, lace flourishing like a rose garden along the edges.

"Do you know what this is?" Laralie asked, fingering the label stuck to the neck of the dress. "It's a Vera Wang dress, from her new limited collection. This has to cost a fortune!"

"Really?" I asked, but... I knew. I'd spent plenty of time as a kid cutting out pictures of these dresses and sticking them to my walls. I didn't want to get into this with her, though. It wasn't important. Not anymore.

Laralie eyeballed me, letting the dress go before sighing. "You have no clue, do you? Alexis, we *work* on magazines that show these dresses off! Have you never noticed?"

I scrunched my shoulders up. "I do desk work, not articles like you." I hated playing dumb, but it was better than explaining what I'd given up on. "It's beautiful, who cares who made it?"

Her lips pouted, a hand dragging over her face. "He's sent you something like this, and you don't even understand." Rubbing her temples, she groaned. "How come guys like this never contact me? *I'd* appreciate it!"

Fidgeting, I brushed the soft material again. "I *do* appreciate it."

"Fine, fine. I guess I'm just a little surprised to see this in person." She reached out, tracing the hem.

When I moved the dress, something slid my way. The small envelope was deliciously familiar, but I didn't want Laralie to see the note. Tucking it into my lap under the desk, I devised a plan to get her to go away so I could read it. Before I could, a new voice spoke out. "Excuse me, Alexis Willow?"

Together, Laralie and I looked up at the man who had appeared. The broadness of his shoulders showing through his tight, black shirt made it clear he took care of himself. There was a two-day-old scruff around his square jaw, heavy bags looking out of place under his sparkling green eyes. Behind his ear sat a simple red pen.

"Yes?" I asked, "I'm Alexis, and you are...?"

"Detective Roose." He extended a large, callused hand. On impulse I shook it, but my skin was numb.

The detective. I'd completely forgotten.

Everyone in the room was staring my way, most didn't bother to be subtle. Roose nodded his head to me. "Could we go somewhere a little more private?"

Laralie made a motion behind his back, pushing up her own boobs while wiggling her hips. I read her lips: "Want me to distract him for you?"

Ducking my head, I quickly shook it. I didn't need her to make this worse. "Sure, we can use one of the conference rooms." I buried the note from Silver in my trouser pocket before I stood.

He ran his thumbs down until they were hooked in his belt. Under one solid arm, a thick folder peeked out. "Lead the way."

On stiff legs, I turned, marching towards the glass-windowed room down the hall. Everyone was still watching me, and when I peered back at Laralie, she held the box up and mouthed, "I'll guard this for you."

Guard it? I knew she was probably going to sit and swoon over the dress, imagining she was wearing it to some fancy party. I was extra glad I'd found the note and took it, it would have been a disaster in her hands.

Opening the door, I motioned Roose inside. He tipped his head, settling at the long table as I closed the shutters. I didn't want my coworkers snooping through the windows at us.

"Sorry about all this," he said as I sat down across from him. His eyes had a wet realness in them that made me think he actually *was* sorry. He pulled out the folder and a notebook. "I'm really hoping you can help me out."

Crinkling my forehead, I sat uncomfortably. "You said this was about Old Stone Bank."

His head bobbed, the red pen twirling in his fingers. I saw how thick they were, as if the young detective had worked on a farm his whole life. "Right. The robbery that happened five years ago. Now, I'm sure you—"

"Is robbery the right word?"

He paused, his pen touching the cover of the notebook. "Excuse me?"

Rocking in place, I shrugged. "I mean, whoever stole all that money... they gave it back to the people it was supposed to go to. Didn't they?"

His smile became very stale, almost patronizing. "Miss Willow, the man who hacked the bank that day, he took what wasn't meant for him. He broke the law. It was a robbery—and a large one. Plain and simple."

Under the table, I pressed a thumb into the back of one hand. "People were being taken advantage of by that insurance company." I'd forgotten the name, it had been so long since the news story had broke.

"I guess you listened to that bullshit spin. Bank Robber Hero," he scoffed. "It's funny. Considering that you were almost killed that day, you're sure happy to defend the criminal we're after."

Killed. That word cut at me, pushing sweat from my pores. Everything about that day had gone fuzzy in my memory, wobbly and muted like it had happened to someone else and I'd only heard the story secondhand.

But he was right, why was I defending someone who'd put people's lives at stake?

My life?

Guilt burned through me, as if someone had put a battery in my chest and sliced it open. "I'm sorry. You're right."

He softened his tone. "That sounded like I was accusing you. I'm not. Actually, I'm here because you're one of the few people who had any contact with the man we're after." His smile was gentle. "I need your help, Miss Willow."

Pushing my hair from my face, I focused on him. "Years ago, when this all went down, I gave my statement. You should have that in your files."

"I do, and I've read it several times." He flicked his notebook open, scanning it. "You didn't have much to say. If anything, you mostly refused to speak. I'm here because I'm hoping to get a clearer picture."

My tongue shriveled. "I don't remember anything. Not really."

The pen twisted faster. "Nothing? How is that possible?"

"After... *it* happened, I went to see a therapist." My mother had insisted. I'd gone from plotting my big plans, to hiding in my room and never leaving the house. "They told me it was a safety mechanism. The trauma kept me from recalling the details."

Roose bent close, grabbing my hands on the table. It made me think of Silver, so I pulled away, uncomfortable with such intimacy from the detective. "Can I show you something?"

I nodded, and he opened up his folder. Sliding a paper to me, he waited anxiously. "Read that and tell me if it means anything to you."

Bending close, I scoured the page. It contained a bunch of symbols, word and number vomit, if you asked me. "What am I looking for?"

"It's right there in the center."

Squinting, I looked... and I saw it. "Oh!" Surprised, I started to read the sentence. It had been hidden in the mess. "It says, 'Silver spoons for some, government cock—" I choked.

The detective was watching me closely, did he want to see my reaction?

Cocks for everyone else, I finished in my head. I flashed him a nervous look. "What is this?"

"It doesn't mean anything to you?"

"It's a little vulgar," I mumbled.

Sighing, he pulled the paper back. "It's a phrase that was hidden in the code that our tech intelligence were able to dig up after the latest hacking attempt. It's the hacker's calling card, if you ask me."

The back of my neck was warm. "Oh," I said simply.

Roose tucked the folder away, his tone stretching like he was begging me. "You honestly have no clue about it, huh?"

"I really don't." I peeked at the door. "Is it alright if I go, now?"

"I wish I had the footage from that day, but it's still tied up in red-tape." His chair squeaked as he rolled it forward, then backwards. In every sense, he was telegraphing his frustration. "Do me one more favor."

"What is it?"

"You think you can't remember anything, but close your eyes and try. I'm counting on you. If you can't give me one tiny bit of info to help close this case... someone else could end up at gun point. And they might not be lucky enough to survive like you did."

It was a hard dose of reality. "Alright," I whispered. My heart was flexing over and over. "I'll try. Is there something in particular you're after?"

"Anything. His face, his voice, just anything."

Scrunching my eyes, I breathed in—held the air. Working through my memory was like digging into a dark cave. I shoved and shoved through the thick black and stifling sand. Somewhere in my skull, there were answers.

In my mind's eye, I glimpsed a gun. It scalded, white hot and aimed at my eye.

Yes.

That was right.

He'd grabbed me, pulled me close, and then he'd whispered... he'd said... Fuck, what had he said. Why had he picked *me*, out of everyone in the bank that day?

My skull was trembling; everything was trembling. I clung to my own arms, hugging tight and fighting off the waves of fear. This was exactly what I'd wanted to avoid. Roose was reminding me of everything I'd buried, forcing it to claw up from the dregs of my mind, making the nightmare real again.

Those eyes...

That voice...

"Miss Willow!"

Roose's palms came down on my shoulders; I'd been about to fall from my seat. Sweat made my shirt cling to me, each breath coming faster and faster.

"Are you okay?" he asked, helping me sit upright.

Firmly, I shoved him away. "Yes, I'm fine." My smile was frail, I knew he wasn't convinced. "This interview is over."

"But Miss—"

"It's over. I can't do this."

Frowning, he moved so I could stand. I held the table, trying to make it clear I was alright without his support. "Please," he said. "I need you to look over some photos. I need answers, clues, anything to help me catch this man before he does this again."

Again.

Laralie's words came back to me. "Did he manage to really do it, hack another bank?"

Roose flinched, considering my question. "No, it was just an attempt through their system. But I'm positive it's the same guy as five years ago."

I was dizzy; I fought not to sit down again. *That man is really back?*

Even though he was still swimming in my vision, I looked at him. "Detective," I said slowly. "Let me give you my cell number. If I think of anything, I'll tell you."

He puffed up, handing me his pen so I could scribble it on the notebook. "Thank you. Here, my card." He slid it from his pocket, offering it to me. "If you don't call me first, I'll reach out to you. If that's okay?"

"Yeah, of course."

His grin was polite, but I knew I'd disappointed him. I would have felt worse about that, except my stomach was still knotting and twisting.

When Roose left the conference room, I darted behind him, hurrying the opposite way towards the restroom. I was on the verge of being sick, the back of my throat itching.

Stumbling against the sink, I spun the knob. Water rushed out, my palms cupping it, splashing my sickly pale skin. In the mirror, I saw how drained I looked. It was as if I'd seen a ghost.

In a way, I did.

Those memories. I just... I didn't want them. I wanted that slice of my life to never float up again. In my pocket, my phone buzzed. Drying my hands, I slid it out, reading the screen.

Silver: Go to Lotus Spa on Fourth Street, they'll be expecting you. Bring the dress, you'll wear it tonight. I'm taking you to dinner.

He'd arranged for me to go to a spa, *and* he wanted to have dinner? I liked that way more than our secret sex club encounter.

I typed back, *Sounds like a date.* Before I hit send, I caught myself smiling in the mirror. Silver had taken me from sick and stressed, to giddy and excited in an instant.

Chuckling, I pushed the button, then put my phone away.

This man...

He made it so easy to forget my troubles.

- Chapter Nine -
Alexis

The spa was on a stretch of downtown that was reserved for high end shops. In other words, a place I rarely explored.

With the box containing my dress under one arm, I strolled through the doors and into the peaceful, wood-wind sounding waiting area. There was a woman at the counter, and she eyeballed me with doubt as I approached.

"Hey there," I said, feeling out of place. "Apparently I have a reservation or something?"

Her drawn on eyebrows moved higher. "Oh?" With long, manicured nails, she flipped the pages of the book on the counter. "Name?"

Could he have picked a snootier spa? "Alexis. Alexis Willow."

She started to smile, but her lips twitched. "Huh. Here you are." She sounded surprised, double checking the list. Then, in a great show of skill, she put on a huge grin and spread her arms. "Welcome to the Lotus Spa! I see you've been booked for the deluxe package."

I gripped the box a tad tighter. "I don't know if I'm a deluxe kind of person."

"Nonsense! It comes with a salt scrub, a manipedi, a sea cucumber soak, and a make-up and hair blow out, as well as a massage!"

It took some effort not to laugh. "Salt and cucumbers? Are you prepping me to be cooked?"

The woman's sour disposition slid back into place. "It's good for your skin. You could use it, honey."

"I... think I'll take the manipedi and the massage, but lets skip the food stuff."

Clearly, she didn't know what to do about being told to take features off. Hovering with her hand by the book, she moved her lips but said nothing.

"Ah," a sweeter voice piped up. Glancing over, I saw a young woman with a blonde bob haircut. She waved, grabbing my free hand gently. "I'm Sarina, I'll be working with you. Come with me, please."

With a final peek at the still scowling host, I nodded. "My pleasure."

Sarina pulled me around a corner, the marble floors echoing as we strolled. Around us, various plants decorated the minimal atmosphere, as did a small river that had been cut into one side of the floor.

The place was gorgeous, I had to admit.

"Here," Sarina said, offering me a robe and some flip-flops as we entered a darker hallway. "Go put these on behind that screen, there's lockers for your items."

I took the robe, testing its soft material. I hadn't expected to change, but it made sense.

"Alright, thanks." I walked behind the tall painted screens. They created tiny cubicles in what had to be a giant changing room.

On one side, I spotted showers. *For after they coat you in salt and seasoning*, I mused. Putting the dress-box in a locker, I started to slide my clothes off. When I tugged at my trousers, I felt something in my back pocket.

Confused, I held up the letter. My heart did a twirl. *I forgot about this!* In all the mess with the detective, I'd blanked on putting away Silver's latest message so no one would see it.

Peeling the note open, I licked my lower lip eagerly.

Dear Pet,

Tonight, I have plans for you. Plans I know you'll love.

I can't wait to share them.

—S

I rubbed the paper, then folded it tight. A long, hot breath escaped me. *Fuck, whatever he writes, it gets me way too excited.* I wondered what he had planned.

I also wondered if I could handle it.

"Miss?" Sarina called out.

"One second!" I stumbled sideways, hurrying to get changed. I put the folded pile of discarded items away with the dress. Then, I tied the robe on securely. It felt amazing on my skin.

She was waiting for me where I'd left her, her hands folded carefully in the pretty floral top she had on. Sarina blended in perfectly with the pretty plants and marbled walls. When she spotted me, her face lit up in a dimpled smile. "You look great."

Self-consciously, I held up my hands. "Hah, I'm the prettiest girl at the Shower Ball."

I expected her to roll her eyes at my stupid joke, but she actually snorted. "Maybe you'll be crowned Queen, then you can wear the shower cap."

Maybe it was her job to be likable, but I didn't care; she was good at it. Laughing, I followed her into a room where a few other women were getting their nails and hair done.

Sarina sat me in a chair; it squished around me, luxuriously plush. "What color would you like on your nails?"

I spread my fingers, frowning. "I don't paint them much. I don't know."

"Here, just look over these and see what catches you." She offered a tray. On top of them, a color wheel of nail polish awaited. I was blown away by the range of choices.

Brushing my hand over the colors, I inhaled. "So many options, huh?"

"Take your time."

I started to thank her for her patience. But then I saw it; the nail polish was glittery, a beam of starlight.

Silver.

Pointing, I controlled my tiny smile. "That one, please."

The manipedi was glorious. I found myself going slack, relaxing as Sarina worked over my fingers and toes. When she was done, I wiggled my nails in awe. They sparkled, a pure silver that was bound to impress.

"You like?" she asked.

"I like. Yeah." They'd match my dress exactly.

"Now, let's do your makeup and hair."

I winced. "This will sound ungrateful, but I'd rather... not."

Sarina tilted her head so fast that her hair swished like a broom. "But you've paid for it."

Silver paid for it. Not me. Shrugging, I blushed nervously. "I haven't been done up like this in—ever, I guess. It's making me feel not very me."

Crouching, she met my eyes with her friendly smile. "I'll only do a little bit. Trust me."

I wanted to say no, but she was so sincere. "Okay. But please don't slather it on."

"I'll make you look like you, just more shiny." She winked, then set about preparing my skin. Sitting there, my relaxing mood diminished. I was wary of what I'd see when she was done.

Except, minutes later, when she told me to open my eyes...

I realized I'd been acting stupid.

"Oh my gosh," I laughed, turning side to side in the mirror. Sarina had kept it simple, just some eye shadow and a little mascara. She'd wound my hair up into a delicate coif, my neck long and exposed. I looked like me, only enhanced. "You're incredible."

Clasping her fingers, she bounced on her heels. "Glad you like it!"

I had a feeling Silver would like the end result, too.

Guiding me further into the building, Sarina waved me into a low-lit room full of candles. It smelled like sandlewood and coconut, a shelf covered in oils taking up a whole wall.

"Just strip your robe off and get under the sheet," she said. "Your massage will start in a few minutes."

"Alright. Sounds wonderful." I could definitely use this massage. The stress from my meeting with detective Roose had left me tense, even if I'd done my best to forget the whole mess.

Sarina slid out the door, so I unbelted my robe, letting it pool at my feet. In just my lavender bra and panties, I snuggled up onto the table. The room was warm, the gentle music making me sleepy.

With my face pushed into the hole at one end of the table, I started to drift off. Distantly I heard the door open, feet scuffing gently my way.

"Welcome back," I mumbled, almost giggling at how drunk I sounded. "I was starting to pass out."

Firm hands slid the sheet down, pressing into my shoulder blades with practiced force. A hot whisper tickled the nape of my neck. "I hope I don't put you to sleep."

I jolted up, nearly banging Silver in the face with my skull. "You!" I gasped, yanking the sheet around my chest.

And it *was* him; he stood there with a wicked smirk, his hands shining from massage oil. He'd rolled his shirt up high to his shoulders, exposing his forearms.

Silver was here.

HERE.

Crossing his biceps, he lifted an eyebrow at me. "You look tense. Let me help."

"How are you here?" I blurted.

"I drove. That's usually how I get around."

"No. *No.* How are you—where's my masseuse?" I was flat out stunned.

He flexed his hands, fingers bending one by one. Fuck, he had beautifully long fingers. "Right in front of you. Though masseur is more correct." He looked me up and down, lingering on my chest through the cloth. "Fancy dress or plain sheet, you manage to be just as stunning."

Being reminded of the Red and Ripe had me squirming. "You planned this all along."

"What, coming here to massage you? Of course."

"Then why that lie about meeting for dinner?" I asked lamely.

He laughed, throwing his head back before leaning close. "That's still happening. But I've been looking forward to this all day. Lie down, Pet."

A tiny spark of desire dazzled into my belly. "You're serious."

"Most of the time." He winked boyishly. "Let me help you relax."

This is going to do the opposite of relaxing me. I inched around slowly, lying on my stomach. The sheet was still clutched around me like armor.

He startled slow; fingers molding against my shoulders. Inching the sheet away, he exposed my spine. My muscles bunched, I wanted to rebel, but his voice stopped me. "Let me do this," he whispered. "Let me take control."

His palms glided downwards, lingering for a moment between my shoulder blades. I was lost in the bliss of his touch. Silver was a master at this, his hands working away my knots, replacing them with something that was slicker... electric.

The sheet was gone, cool air tickling across my hips and ass. I turned, wanting to say how he shouldn't, how I wasn't ready.

Like silk, he pressed down to the backs of my knees. I jumped, and his chuckle was hot chocolate in my veins. He cupped my calves, digging in until he was stroking the soles of my feet. It was gradual, but the flames of arousal began to lick at me.

"Is that good?" he asked.

Chewing my lip, I shoved my head into the forehead rest. My muffle of agreement must have pleased him, because he swung across me, dragging his fingertips along the muscles of my arms. With each stroke, my nerves turned from arching cats into purring kittens.

Then he slid his hand up the inside of my thigh, ruining everything.

"Hey!" I gasped, pushing up on my hands to stare at him.

His eyes twinkled. "Something wrong?"

"I don't want a happy ending with this massage."

"Everyone wants a happy ending," he said softly, bending away so I couldn't tell what the expression on his face meant. The low lights hid him from me, and worse, I sensed him pulling away.

Before I could investigate what was wrong, Silver peered back at me. The glimmering centers of his amber eyes were unforgettable. He was here—with me—and I convinced myself whatever I'd sensed was my imagination. "Don't lie," he said. "It's obvious you want me to touch you."

I bristled, not just because of his audacity, but because he was right. "You're the one who showed up out of nowhere to give me a massage. If anyone wants anything here, it's you."

"Oh, you're definitely right," he chuckled. His weight settled on the table, his palms on either side of my hips. The candles along the walls turned his skin into a glistening bronze canvas. "I want to touch you more than anything, I want to feel the soft folds around your clit and discover how *wet* I'm getting you, Pet."

My breath hitched, become a solid ball in my throat. Silver lifted a hand in the air, flexing his fingers. On impulse, my pussy clenched. "Are you asking me to stop?"

"I'm just saying I'm not... ready for you to go that far."

Smiling so his teeth didn't show, Silver motioned for me to turn back around. "I have a feeling you're more ready than you realize."

Rubbing my lower back, he blew air on the side of my throat. "Let me show you."

Closing my eyes, I sucked in through my nose. That was my only response.

It was enough.

He bent over the edge of the table, his weight pressing the heels of his palms into my shoulders. Small circles, rhythmic motions, Silver touched me with precision. His fingers swept down my ribs, grazing the outsides of my breasts.

I was breathing faster, wiggling in place the longer I endured his touch. He acted like he knew my body already. How could he? What allowed him to be so perfect in drawing out the heat in my lower belly?

Experience, I thought to myself. Someone as sexy as him must have had many other partners. I'd seen the sex club he liked to attend. But I didn't want to think about that—I wanted to focus on Silver and how he made me *feel*.

Good.

No. Wonderful.

Panting, I shivered at the way his nails scraped over my spine. He reached the crest of my ass, then dodged around it, not touching me. My disappointment was crisp, I even groaned.

His strained hiss made my hair stand on end.

My desire was lightning in a bottle, and he'd popped the cork. He was proving he could turn me on, make me want his touch.

Lying on that massage table, my thighs shaking as arousal flooded my cells, I felt panic. I was vulnerable like this, at the mercy of someone who was making me crave erotic, terrible things.

I wanted him to stop teasing me. I wanted him to quit stopping short of the gap between my legs. His teeth brushed my temple. "The heat coming off of your pussy is burning the air around my hand," he whispered.

Rocking my hips, I pushed into his palm; he squeezed my ass and I moaned. It was unconscious, and I couldn't take it back.

"That sound is driving me fucking insane," he growled. "My cock is throbbing, Pet."

I was hit with the compelling desire to see that. How incredible would he look, his shaft swollen, flexing to its full length. If he slid his pants down, right now, would I be able to resist touching him?

Tasting him?

"Enough," he said. Firm fingers wrapped in my hair, pulling it from its neat little up-do. Silver contorted me around, straddling my waist as he yanked my mouth to his. He'd spun me so fast my back cracked, the noise cascading through the room.

The only other noise was my desperate whimper.

We kissed like that for an unknown stretch of time. It could have been minutes, it could have been centuries. In just a sheet and lingerie, I curled into his arms. Silver pushed a palm along my ribs, snaking it between my thighs.

Heaven help me, I started to spread them.

Wait, I warned myself. *Not here. It can't be here.* Sex in a public place wasn't something I could ever do. I wasn't brave enough, or bold enough.

But he must be.

Silver was wild, he was going to be disappointed with someone like me.

"Stop," I said, my voice cracking.

He chuckled darkly against my neck. My blush went full body, but I kept from wilting. Silver's hand lazily stroked up my bare knee...

161

then away. "I'm pushing you too fast, is that it?"

Tugging the sheet up to my neck, I held still. Maybe he'd sit with me here, just holding me, even if I didn't want to fuck. "Sort of. I don't know. I'm just not sure I can do this whole thing here."

"Here, as in this building?" Tucking some of my hair behind my ear, he grinned. "Or here, as in fucking me at all. You keep stopping me from going further."

I started to stutter; I hated the idea that he'd think I didn't *want* him. "No! It's not that I don't want to do... that." Steeling myself, I glanced down at the front of his pants. His hard-on was massive, and when he saw me look, he smirked even bigger. "I'm not making out with you half-naked because I'm not into you, Silver."

Cupping my chin, he closed the gap between us. "I'm only teasing. It's obvious you want me." His voice dropped an octave, his free hand massaging his cock through his pants. "And it's clear I want *you*."

Fixated on his erotic gesture, I froze. It was like my brain had the hiccups.

He said, "Let's get out of here. It's close to our dinner reservation, anyway." He abandoned me, but I took cruel solace in the way he grunted at his uncomfortable erection. I'd seen the shape of it so many times, I was starting to get an idea of its size.

Big.

That was a perfectly good word for it.

"Go change into your outfit." He washed his hands in the nearby sink. "I'll wait for you by the front desk."

The warm room had become smoldering. It was a relief when I escaped down the hall, my lungs able to take in a full breath finally. *Will he be like that every time? So hungry, so tempting?*

I knew the answer.

As long as I resisted him, he'd keep pushing.

What would happen when I finally gave in?

- Chapter Ten -

Alexis

"You seem a little different," he said.

Silver had driven us over to the restaurant, a fast trip from the spa. Before our escape, Sarina had spotted me in the hallway. Her eyes had met mine, curious but not cutting. She must have been thinking about what Silver and I had been up to.

After all, I still was.

Now, leaning into the booth, I sipped my cocktail too fast. "Different than what? The first time we met up, I wasn't exactly in my element."

Considering my question, he lingered on it more than seemed right. Then he shook his head, mouth turning into a half frown. "In general. It's like your mind isn't fully here."

He's right, I thought sullenly. A sliver of my brain had been focused on my meeting with

Detective Roose. He'd crept into my life like a black beast from an old nightmare. Everything had been going so great, I didn't want to dredge up my damn history from five years back.

I won't let that guy ruin my mood. Forcing a smile, I gave Silver my most brash grin. "Maybe I'm just thinking about all the amazing things you've done for me."

"You mean you've been enjoying my gifts."

"Very much so." I lifted a finger, brushing one of the mercury-folds of my gown pointedly.

"I'm glad," he said softly. "But I wonder if you've enjoyed *all* of my gifts?"

It took me a second, but the wolfish edge to his mouth gave him away. I knew what he was referring to, and it made my knees push together. Oh yes, I'd 'enjoyed' the special vibrator he'd sent my way. Shit, was my whole face glowing red?

Winking, he sipped from his glass. "I'm proud of that toy. I spent a while designing it."

"Is that what you do?" I asked, leaping at any info about him. "You design—ah, sex toys?" My blush was growing hotter.

"I do a lot of things, my hands are in a few companies. I like to stay busy."

"You mean you run *multiple* businesses?" My eyes popped wide. "That sounds exhausting." It also explained his obvious income.

Silver cocked his head. "I have a partner. He helps run things behind the scenes, the less exciting areas."

That word, 'exciting.' It had me thinking about the vibrating purple dildo all over again. "I can't get over the fact that you sell..." I covered one side of my mouth. "Sex toys."

He waved his hand in the air. "I don't sell *toys*. I design an interaction. An encounter.

I want to make sure whoever uses them remembers the experience that *I* gave them."

His eyes focused on me, catching fire as the chandelier glinted off of them.

I swallowed and mumbled, "That's kind of arrogant."

His face fell, and I realized what I'd said. I winced, but he cut off my explanation with a loud laugh. Holding his forehead, he peeked at me through his fingers. His smile was raw, real. "That's more like it. I love that kind of honesty."

Fidgeting, I finished my drink and willed another to appear from thin air. "What I meant was—"

"Don't apologize." He lowered his voice. "It *is* arrogant. That's who I am. I know what I want, and usually... I can figure out what other people want." His fingers crossed over, brushing mine. "Did you come while thinking about me?"

My brain sizzled, white hot energy stealing my thoughts.

"That good?" he asked. "Wait until you play with the real thing."

I rocked on my chair, enjoying the pressure that came from scissoring my thighs. I was still buzzing from his sensual massage, but more than that, he was getting into my head.

Just like with his very first letter.

"Who are you?" I whispered.

He gripped my wrist, his sinful aura covering me. "I'm the man who's going to fuck you until you see stars. When I take you, it won't be with just my mouth. Or my hands. Or my cock. I'm going to make you mine down to your very soul. And then I'm going to go even deeper."

It was a wonder that I could keep from gasping out loud. My nipples were tingling from how solid they were, rubbing at the gown's material. I felt like one big, pulsing vein, everything was connected to the shaking muscles in my lower belly.

I said, "I meant what kind of man are you. Who sends packages to a stranger, who takes someone to a sex club? This money, this attention... I don't understand you."

"Of course you do." His fingers trailed down my arm, but they never left. "You understand who I am because you're the same as me."

That made my spine go stiff. "I'm nothing like you," I laughed bitterly. "I'm plain, I'm boring. The most exciting part of my day used to be when a new show I could marathon dropped on Netflix."

Silver breathed out, managing to bring his face ever closer to mine. I could see nothing but him. "You're exactly like me, Pet, otherwise you wouldn't be here. But if you doubt this side of you... the brave and curious part that would go to a sex club, or fantasize about someone while grinding on a vibrator he's sent her…"

Fuck, could I be any redder?

He said, "If you're confused, then maybe we should help you find out how far you're willing to go." His teeth flashed, and I imagined them on my jaw. "Let me help you understand who you are."

My voice sounded like a breeze through a corn field. "What do you mean?"

"You could have backed out of everything… if you really wanted to. But you didn't. I want to see where your desires truly lie, what darkness lives deep in your bones, what wickedness sleeps in your core."

Silver wanted to prove to me that I was like him.

Was he right?

"Well?" he asked softly, his voice searing me. "Do you want to test your tastes in public or private?"

From the corner of my eye, I saw the waiter approaching. I had the uneasy sense that if he reached us, this moment would be gone. Not just gone, but erased from my memory—from my potential future. If I didn't answer now, I'd go back to my boring world.

I forced my voice to remain steady. "Private."

He smiled, dropping a wad of cash onto the table.

The waiter froze, pulling up short. "Sir," he asked, "Aren't you going to order dinner?"

"No," Silver said, taking my hand and leading me to my shaking feet. "I've been saving my appetite for something else."

I wondered if this man might actually eat me alive.

And if I would even stop him.

- Chapter Eleven -

Alexis

The building we pulled up to was like a slab of golden granite in the middle of the city. It jutted up and away into the night's void. So much of it was glass that I wondered if anyone living here could have any privacy.

Silver parked his car out front, guiding me towards the entrance where a doorman waited in a black cap and gloves. The man didn't do much beyond glancing at us, then he waved us inside with a deep nod to Silver.

"You must be important," I said.

"Maybe." He tapped the elevator, sliding into the too-small pocket with me. In that space, I held my breath and waited.

What was I waiting for?

For him to touch me.

To kiss me.

To make good on his promise that he'd

show me what it'd feel like to come for him, and not just his sex-toy-gift.

But Silver did nothing, he just leaned on the reflective walls and watched me as if he could read my mind. I didn't even see him blink.

Was he holding his breath like me?

I filled my lungs, catching some of his alluring scent just as the doors dinged open. Stumbling out, I felt his hand on my elbow, steadying me. It was electric, and I had to move away before my senses fried.

He smiled knowingly at me, but by then, I'd noticed my surroundings.

"The elevator goes right to your apartment?" I whispered, stunned by the cavernous penthouse.

"I own the whole building," he said casually. "But yes, that elevator brings me right here. Nice and close to my bed." His chuckle was velvet on my neck.

As late as it was, the city was a field of sparklers through the full circle of windows. Beyond, I glimpsed the telltale curve of the Fremont bridge.

"This is gorgeous," I said honestly.

"No." He hadn't stopped staring at me, not since dinner.

Not since he'd met me.

He said, "You're what's gorgeous."

Grabbing the edge of what had to be a pure crystal table, I stared at him. My heart had swung upwards, a pendulum that kept blocking my words. Finally, I laughed. "Don't tease me."

"I'm not." His single step forward was as loud as a gong. "But I can, if you'd like. Fuck, now all I can picture is spreading you out on my bed, making you beg me to lick that sweet pussy of yours."

He inhaled sharply, and I mimicked him. My hip bumped the table. "Could I have a drink?" *Before we go further*, was my unsaid

175

thought.

Silver cracked a grin, sliding his tie looser around his neck. "Of course." The room was designed to be large and open, I could watch him sway all the way to the kitchen, his fingers snatching two glasses from a shelf.

I used the brief escape from his nearness to gather my strength. It was as if this man had his delicious hands wrapped right around my rib cage, squeezing without even touching me.

Silver came back, the lights along the wide windows creating patterns on his white shirt. His muscles strained, hidden like beasts below the ocean. I watched them writhe, imagined him holding me as his smirk brushed my mouth.

"Here," he said, handing me a glass full of topaz liquid. "Riesling. My favorite."

I didn't care what it was, I just took a deep swig. The acid-burn helped clear my throat, but it muddled my thoughts. "You really live here?"

"Do you think I broke into someone else's home?" He grinned, one arm straining his shirt as he pointed at the high ceilings. "Which part of me seems like a lie? My money, my perverse hobbies... or something else?"

Squinting at him, I bit the edge of my own lip. "Your name."

Something dark rippled across his face. A drink from his glass smoothed it away. "Let me give you a tour, Pet."

My steps echoed on the hardwood floors. Soon, they were replaced by gorgeous white rugs. He showed me the gigantic dining area, the table set for five people, though I had trouble picturing anyone ever entering Silver's home.

I was still struggling with the fact *I* was here.

He let me peek into his private office, the desk strewn with sketches and notes, many which were clearly sex toys. Silver even gave me a tour of the roof.

The wind teased my hair from its loose bun. I went to fix it, but his hand on my elbow stopped me. "Wait," he whispered, his voice heating me in the cool night. "Leave it down. I like it messy."

I could see the blink of stars just beyond his ear. They were lost in a sky that was too black to be real. How funny was it that I found him more entrancing than those ancient lights?

His fingers linked with mine. "Follow me."

Deep down, I knew where we were going.

Silver pulled me back inside, into a room as wide as the living area. The walls were richly metallic and black, the king bed's blankets matching. The rug was so dense I had to make sure I wasn't walking on fuzzy pillows.

I'd never seen such a luxurious

bedroom. One wall was cut in an arch, a black marble bathroom with a giant open shower waiting beyond. There were steps leading to a platform with a jacuzzi.

Fingers came down on my shoulders from behind. All at once, the tension in the air shifted. Silver took my wine glass, but I didn't see where he dropped it.

"I'm done holding back," he said.

Every hair on my body stood tight. He traced down my arms, his hips pressing into my ass. I was too aware of how thin the dress he'd given me was. It offered no protection, my nipples outlined through the fabric.

In the mirror across the way, I saw how pursed my lips were. I was gasping soundlessly, pink and excited. Silver's affect on me was clear as crystal.

His lips traced the jewel in my earlobe. "I love seeing you draped in my gifts."

Closing my eyes, I swayed. He didn't

need to cut me open to steal my strength, he was forcing it out of me with every word.

Hot, wet lips came down on my neck. Instantly I groaned, bending at the knee as the sensation rocked me at my core. He made a similar sound, speaking against my skin as his hands gripped me against him. "Don't try and deny it. You're getting turned on, you've wanted to do this for some time with me. Haven't you, Pet?"

Swallowing, I said, "I wouldn't lie. I couldn't."

"No," he agreed, tracing down the front of my dress as I whimpered. "You couldn't."

Champagne-like bubbles fizzed through my thighs, honing in on my pussy. I pulled at his hands, spinning to face him. Down and up and everything else blurred so that there was only his mouth and mine.

Silver kissed me hard enough to push me down into the mattress. The plush cover cradled me, contrasting against his solid body. There was no escaping him, he was as immovable as a freight train. *I don't want him to move,* I thought through my murky haze. *I want him to keep kissing me until my face is too numb to feel it.*

Teeth grazed my chin, my shoulder; the expensive gown exploded as he ripped the straps away. I *felt* his energy, and I felt how he didn't give a shit about the money he'd just thrown away.

This man cared only about *me.*

"I've wanted to do this for so long," he growled. His lips plucked over my collar bone, playing me like an instrument. "So long, you don't even know."

I shivered, trying to focus on him but only seeing his glossy hair. "But it hasn't even been that long."

The massive weight of him paused. I strained, arching up to get more of his mouth.

He moved enough to watch me, and in the curling smoke of his eyes, I saw something so familiar it made me freeze. Why did I feel like I recognized that look?

"It has," he said flatly.

There was an almost tangible memory out of my reach, and I thought, if I focused, I could pull it from my skull. All I needed was a clear mind.

Silver had no intentions of giving me that.

The bed shifted as he suddenly leaned away. Propping on my elbows, I reached for him, eager to get his heat back. The slip of a smile he wore grew larger. "One second." He reached for the bedside table, tugging open a small drawer in the lacquered black wood.

Craning my neck, I tried to see what he was getting. *Maybe it's a condom.* A flash of trepidation wormed into my guts. I wanted this, I knew I did, but every step that brought it closer was terrifying.

Then I saw the red silk straps.

"Lean back," he said, motioning.

Licking my lower lip, I stayed where I was. "What are those for?"

Silver showed me the most cutting smirk. "To bind you, Pet. I want to make you feel amazing, but on my terms."

A hard pressure made me crunch together. My knees touched my shoulders, my skin vulnerable with the dress shredded. He was into bondage, so what? It wasn't that surprising, so why the hell was my brain screaming at me not to let him do this?

I don't like being confined.

Trapped.

He knelt beside me, and through the raging eagerness in his stare, I sensed his patience. "I won't hurt you," he promised.

And it *was* a promise.

There's a chance I was insane to let him

do this to me. And there was a good chance I was going to look back on this and wonder what the hell had gotten into me.

But when I raked my eyes over his face, considered the set of his jaw... the way he held himself at bay... I couldn't fight my curiosity. He'd told me he wanted to test how deep my own wickedness went.

Wouldn't backing out now waste that chance?

Lifting my wrists, I crossed them together. "Like this?"

Silver's groan was primal. "Just the sight of you doing that is making my cock throb."

A tiny whimper slipped through my lips. Grabbing my hands, he pulled them over my head. The position stretched me out, my chest rolling high, my nipples burning with desire against my dress. He was fast, efficient; in seconds, he'd bound my wrists together on the metal bed-frame.

Sitting back, he lingered on watching me. The fire in his amber eyes brushed every part of my body. Where he looked, I felt his touch. The air vibrated, alive with our expectations.

Both of us were waiting.

Hooking his fingers into his jacket and tie, he fished them over his head. My heart began to race as he flicked his buttons, peeling his dress-shirt open to expose his torso. His muscles were as defined as steps in a mountain, the edges shadowed and leading me down.

I could see the outline of his cock, seconds before he made it even easier through his tight briefs. There was a damp spot, and my clit swelled as I understood. *Precome.* He was as excited as I was.

Silver slid his palms upwards, draping across my body to grip my wrists. He squeezed, breathing in while I moaned. The wetness of his seeking mouth conquered mine. Slipping around firmly, his tongue pressed down, trapping mine as surely as he'd trapped the rest of me.

The unbreakable shield of his chest ground along my front. In a single swipe, he yanked the dress down, popping my bra free. My panties were ripped to my knees. There was nothing between us but skin and unspoken words.

I was on the verge of calling his name, and he... I'm not sure. I only sensed there was something on the tip of his tongue.

Instead of speaking, he kissed me again.

Fingertips smoothed over my pussy lips, up and down. Spreading me, he dipped into the wetness he'd created. "You're dripping," he whispered.

Burying himself in me up to the knuckle, he pushed against my warm walls. "Ah!" I gasped, my knees scraping together. He was testing how sensitive I was, the roof of my pussy already tingling with rawness.

I was hyper aware of his every motion, my heart leaping—my thighs shaking. Lowering himself, he rolled his tongue over my exposed clit. I jumped; he did it again, licking quicker.

The straps curled against my wrists. "That's too much," I whimpered.

Silver glanced up at me, his face hidden by my pussy, but I *felt* his expression.

That smirk cut over my flesh, then it buried on my twitching clit all over again. Straining against my bonds, I worked to hold back a desperate moan. When he bent his fingers inside of me, adding a third, I lost the battle.

"Fuck," I sobbed, arching like a bridge in the wind. "Silver—please!"

All at once he stopped everything. It was so abrupt that I thought something must be wrong. Looking down my sweating body, I stared into his burning eyes. "Beg me," he said, breathing heavily. He looked delirious. "Tell me you need me to let you come."

If I wasn't already flushing, I would have started. "Beg you?"

Gripping my ankles, he threw my legs over his shoulders. My pussy was trapped inches from his smile. "Beg me," he commanded, "Or I'll take you to the edge of orgasm and never let you over."

As turned on as I was, this demand made me squirm awkwardly. "I don't think I can."

"You can." His thumbs peeled my lower lips wide. "You will," he said, the syllables tickling my skin. "Maybe you just need some motivation."

His tongue lapped at me, a starving man sitting before a feast. The tip would firmly circle my clit, making me gyrate helplessly. Each time I shook, tensing on the brink of coming, he'd retreat and kiss my inner thighs, or my knee, or any place else.

Sweat ran down into my eyes. It collected across my breasts, dripping into my bellybutton. The tension in my muscles was starting to hurt, everything as stiff as steel beams. In a short time—had it been short?—he'd made my body feel like I'd been struggling through a marathon.

But still, he kept the finish line out of reach.

Boiling, I grit my teeth and tossed my head. "Stop teasing me, please!" I shouted.

"Fuck, say please again. That's what I want to hear."

Silver wrapped his lips around my cunt, suckling gingerly. My orgasm danced on the fringe of my vision, it corrupted my damn mind with desperation. I could buck and strain all I wanted, but he'd just inch away, my swollen pussy robbed of contact.

I shattered. "Please!" I sobbed, nearly incoherent. "Let me come, let me finish, fucking let me just come! Silver, please! *Please!*"

Instead of release, he stopped touching me entirely.

Gasping, I stared at him in disbelief. He was kneeling over me, a foil packet shredding in his fingers. In spite of his calm movements, I could feel the lust coming off of him in waves. It made the air heavy, pressing me further into the soaked blankets.

Silver slid the condom down his shaft with practiced ease. He flipped me on my belly, the straps binding my skin tighter. "I'm going to fuck you now." His palm ran down my vertebrae, capturing one of my ass cheeks and digging in. "I'm going to bury my cock into you inch by fucking inch. Then I'm going to do it again. And again. And again. Until you forget your name, thinking of yourself entirely as mine, and no one else's."

I was holding my breath. What was I supposed to say?

He pressed the head of his cock against my pussy. If he wanted a response from me, he didn't wait to hear it.

The first thrust stretched me dangerously. The tip of his length filled me, dragging along my flexing inner walls. Pushing my face into the pillow, I gripped at the bed-frame. I couldn't manage much with my wrists tied, my fingers were barely hooking on. I needed every fragment of control I could find.

"Ah!" I gasped, a thrill running through me when I felt him slide fully into place. My ears were ringing, a blackness creeping around my vision. Was I losing focus from pleasure, or because I kept forgetting to take in a full breath?

Then he leaned forward, holding my hips to move me how he wanted. Withdrawing with the patience of a saint, he lingered with just the head of his cock inside of me.

The next thrust shook the whole fucking bed.

I'd thought recently about how long it had been since I'd last had sex. It was a frail memory, at best. With each stroke, Silver was dissolving the experience of every other man. He was imprinting himself on me, and if I'd doubted it was possible, I knew better now.

Reaching between us, he leaned forward and kissed the nape of my neck. Strong fingers found my clit, strumming it without slowing down his pace. "Talk to me," he instructed. "Tell me how this feels."

"Amazing!" I breathed, clutching to the sound of my own voice. "Good, so damn good. Please, let me come, I need to fucking come so bad!"

His teeth brushed my earlobe. "I know."

He was acting so calm, but with every

motion of his cock inside of me, I sensed his composure fraying. It started slow, a loose thread that was swaying in the wind. But then those threads caught on something—it was sharp, and surprising, and I dared to hope it was *me.*

I wanted to be the event that shook Silver to his core.

My brief, proud hope became a real possibility when his breath turned ragged in my ears. He was a steam engine, pounding down my tracks and not showing a hint of slowing down.

Under his perfect touch, my clit throbbed. The pressure built back to where it had been when he was eating me out. He whispered, "I can feel how hot you are. Your pussy is burning up, fuck, you feel fantastic."

Swooning, I closed my eyes and bit into the pillow. His cock swelled, stunning me as it battled between pleasure and pain. But was this pain? It was too muddled, I didn't even care that he was clutching my hip so hard there would definitely be bruises.

I was hovering on the edge of coming. It was right there, right fucking there.

What was missing?

"Come for me," he growled in my ear.

Groaning so fiercely that it turned into a scream, my body became one big knot. My pussy milked him, tingles rolling from my lower belly to my brain. I'd never had an orgasm that went so *deep.*

Panting, I hung on just enough to rock my hips back onto him. He didn't expect that; shocking him was almost as good as coming.

His lips touched the edge of the emerald earring. The reminder of how we'd gotten here —the mysterious letters, the little games—sent me over the edge again.

"Fuck," I managed, though it hardly sounded like a word. I was buzzing with delight, still riding the crest of orgasm when he started to shake.

"I'm so close," he whispered. "Fuck, so damn close. Do you want me to come inside of you, Pet?" His shaft flexed, drilling harder, rubbing the roof of my pussy.

I'd lost the power of language, but my plaintive whimper was enough for him. He pulled his other hand away from my clit, gripping my waist as he slammed into me with new energy.

I felt his orgasm through his fingertips first. They vibrated, his muscles hardening more than his cock was. Buried in me to his root, his cock jerked. Through the condom, I felt the quake of his powerful climax. I worried he'd break the condom; how could he not?

Shuddering, he stroked slower—finally just holding me steady. Though he was done, the air in the room hadn't changed. This moment felt more important than it should have. Wasn't this just sex?

Then why did it seem like so much more?

Silver brushed his hand through my hair. "That was amazing. I don't want to untie you," he said without a hint of irony.

It should have been scary, except it wasn't. I blamed it on how dazed I was, my body and mind languishing from pleasure.

My wrists were jostled; he was freeing me. Flipping over, I looked up at him and smiled. He was naked, and it was glorious. I watched as he rolled the condom up, walking across to the bathroom to dispose of it.

"I've never done anything like that. I mean, especially not with a stranger," I laughed self-consciously.

Silver stood in the doorway, a figure so beautiful and dark. He seemed cut from another time, more comfortable in the pages of an old novel than in front of my eyes.

He stepped forward, and I fidgeted at his approach. The blankets caved under him, his arm weaving around my middle, forcing my spine against his chest. His heart was reverberating; he was laughing, but not nervously like I had been.

"Stranger," he said, letting the word roll over his tongue like he was chewing a piece of candy. "Do I really feel like a stranger?"

I twisted, searching his eyes. "I don't know. You're sort of like... a concept I've heard of, but never experienced myself." Smiling shyly, I traced his shoulder. Touching him like this was a gift I didn't want to lose. "Familiar, but entirely unknown. Does that sound weird?"

"It's not weird, no."

Under my nails, his rich tattoos were shiny with sweat. "It's different for you though, isn't it?" I flicked my eyes up. "You treat me— my body... like you know it already."

Silver held my eyes, steady and amused.

"I did say I knew you better than you realized."

My laugh was too loud, too nervous. "I don't know why you keep saying that."

He ran a finger down my bare shoulder, lifting goosebumps. "Because it's true. Your tastes, your preferences, the dips and curves of your perfect body." He constricted around me like living rope. "You finally belong to me, Pet. I'm never letting you go."

- Chapter Twelve -

Alexis

I scrambled, my mind on autopilot. He was telling me that he *knew* me. That I belonged to him?

Silver really *had* been stalking me.

That was it. How else could he know things like my shoe size... where I lived... where I worked? And why had I given that all a pass until now? Why had I let myself be so damn naive?

Every built in fear that had chased me since five years ago kicked in. Stalkers were dangerous, and danger was something I'd taken painful steps to always avoid. *Why was I so stupid?*

I didn't know I was standing until Silver reached for me, holding me by my arms and keeping me from collapsing to the floor. "Pet?" he asked.

I couldn't answer, I just swayed.

I'm insane, he's insane.

What if he ties me up and keeps me here forever... he said he wanted to... what if he hurts me... what if...

"Pet! Are you alright?" He shook me, demanding I look at him, and still... I could only close my eyes. This wasn't real, this wasn't possibly real, this...

"Alexis!"

My eyes popped open, fixing in shock on Silver. His face was tormented, fine lines and a deep furrow on the bridge of his nose. I'd never seen him so worried. It would have been comforting if I wasn't so freaked out.

I pushed backwards, hugging my naked chest. "Tell me what's going on." My voice was shaking; I tensed, making myself harden. This time, my words were sharp and solid. "Who the hell *are* you?"

Silver lifted his hands, spreading his

fingers. "Calm down."

"I'm not going to calm down!" I couldn't, the anger was all that was keeping me together. I latched onto it, desperate to stay on my feet. "This is a sick game, stalking someone and playing with them! I don't get it... I don't..." *I let him get too close to me.*

That time, when he reached for me, I backed away. I was moving too quick, my body like a broken marionette. I swung one way, my hip slamming into the bedside table. The bolt of pain made me wince, but it was the reminder of how he'd clung to my skin while burying his cock in my depths.

I'd let a mad man tie me up. I'd fucked someone crazy enough to follow me around for who knew who long, and I'd justified all of it. But his threat of keeping me here, of capturing me so I could never leave—that had been too much.

Grabbing my dress, I started to slide it

on. The top was ruined, it wouldn't keep me decent. Silver moved my way, I gave him a warning look. Instead of grabbing at me, he scooped his jacket off the floor, holding it out.

Warily I took it, sliding the heavy material around my body. It was saturated with his scent. It reminded me wretchedly of the first night we'd met. He'd given me his jacket to keep me warm... to protect me. As much as I didn't want it to, it made me feel safe.

A mountain was growing up and out of me. The pressure crushed my soul.

On bare feet I rushed towards the elevator. I didn't look back, it was an impossible task. If I just kept my eyes forward, I could make it out of this alive.

Before I could get into the sliding doors, he swiped out his palm and caught the edge, blocking me from entering. "Wait!" he growled, his fury rivaling my terror. "Just wait a fucking minute."

Gritting my teeth, I ducked under his arm.

Amazingly, he didn't reach for me. I faced the glass windows, eyeing the city outside and willing myself to transport away from here. *This is too much, I don't understand any of this! I need air, I need to get out!*

Something solid landed by my feet, startling me. Glancing down, I saw it was my purse. Silver said, "Don't forget that. You'll need your phone to reach me."

The elevator doors pinched together before I could reply. I didn't even know what I would have said, because honestly, I wasn't sure if I wanted to see this crazy man again.

It was raining outside. The doorman was taking shelter under the eaves when I burst past him. "Hey!" he shouted after me.

I didn't slow down.

Why did he pick me?

My bare heels splattered over the shining asphalt.

Why?

Headlights beamed at me, my lungs shredding from exertion.

WHY?

Cement bit into my feet, a slippery patch making me stumble. Clutching the jacket, I crumbled into a heap, my knees skidding and bleeding. A distant roar, like a coming tornado, filled my ears. I couldn't hear the cars, the horns, or the lingering people wandering in the night air.

Shaking so hard I expected my bones to come undone, I hugged my knees. Maybe I was crying, maybe it was the rain. It didn't even matter. There was no making sense of what had happened back there.

You should be scared, I told myself. Lifting my chin an inch, I glared at my raw knees. *No. You should be pissed.* Silver wasn't just some distant admirer. He was a bastard who'd led me into a game where he could conquer me, break me down, and keep me at his side.

But why pick me? It made no fucking sense!

"Are you alright?"

My head jerked up; I'd been picturing Silver so clearly that I expected him to be the one speaking. Instead, a police officer with a flashlight crouched over me. He offered a hand, shining the light in my eyes. "Did someone assault you? Are you injured?"

Swallowing, I let him help me to my feet. "I'm fine," I lied.

He glanced down at my bare feet pointedly.

I smiled, but it was frail and ready to crack. "I left my shoes at a... friend's place."

The cop clearly read 'friend' as hookup. His eyebrow quirked, his look of worry turning into one of amused defeat. I wasn't the only girl he'd find tonight doing a walk of shame.

"Let me give you a ride," he sighed, thumbing at his parked car.

I came close to saying no. Overhead, thunder rampaged through the blackening clouds. I couldn't walk home the way I was, and taking a taxi didn't offer the same comfort as a police escort. I had no clue if Silver might come after me.

He knew where I lived, after all.

With a sheepish nod, I let the cop open the rear door of his car for me.

"It's messy out there," he said, settling in the front. His hooded eyes peeked at me through the rear-view mirror. "I'm Officer Santile."

Fingering the pockets of the jacket, I hunched my shoulders. "Alexis. Alexis Willow."

I sounded too forlorn. His forehead crinkled. "You sure you're alright, Miss Willow?"

Not at all. "Yeah. Just a long evening."

Officer Santile turned the engine over, leaving me to wallow. And I *would* have wallowed, I was in prime woe-is-me mode.

Inside the jacket pocket, something poked my finger.

Curious, I slid the tiny card into the air. There wasn't much light in the car, just the lazy bursts as we passed by buildings or other vehicles. It was enough, though, for me to read the words on the piece of stiff paper.

Keswick Silverwell

CEO of Pure Pleasure Inc.

1223 Avelera Ave, Portland OR

I breathed in through my nose, loud enough that Santile peered at me. "Ma'am?"

It's his business card. It has to be! Holy shit. Shaking myself, I stuttered, "I'm fine. Everything is fine back here."

Tracing the edge of the card, I experienced my stomach flipping. I knew his name. I knew his actual fucking name. I even knew where he worked!

So what? The tiny voice in my skull buzzed. *It doesn't matter. You don't want to see him again!* What good could come from interacting with a guy like him?

As if on cue, his scent wafted off of the jacket. A helpless flutter traveled into my scraped knees. It was too easy to be reminded of what it had been like to be so close to him. How he'd teased me, bound me, made me come while his cock drove into me at full capacity.

Keswick Silverwell.

I had so many questions I wanted answers to.

Would I ever get them?

"Have a good night," the cop said as he pulled outside my home.

Climbing from the car, I shivered at the cold puddles around my ankles. "Thanks for the ride."

"You sure you're alright?"

Considering his question, I came close to asking him to stay nearby. If I said I had a stalker, would he believe me? Wouldn't I have to give him the name of the man who might show up here?

Deep down, I realized I didn't want to get Silver in trouble.

I really *was* fucked up.

"I'm fine. Thank you again." Turning, I ran up to my door. But here's the truth. As much as I didn't want to cause harm to Silver... I still took my phone out, dialing most of the emergency number before stalking around my house with a baseball bat in hand.

I was alone.

Except for my torrent of thoughts... I was alone.

****

Water hit me in the face.

"Hey!" I shouted, gaping at Laralie.

Her face pinched in, no humor in her usually cheery features. "Talk to me."

It had been three days since I'd last seen Silver. Or Keswick. I didn't know what to call him anymore. Either way, Laralie had sensed my brooding mood—not that I'd been subtle—and asked me out to lunch.

I was regretting agreeing to it, especially as she sat across from me, her straw at the ready. Pushing my half-eaten sandwich away, I sighed. "There's nothing to talk about—ah!" She'd flicked more water; I hastily wiped it from my shirt. "Laralie, come on."

"I gave you fair warning. *Talk to me,* or be water boarded!"

"This is unnecessary torture!"

"Only if you keep resisting!"

Throwing my hands up, I rolled my eyes. "Okay, okay! I surrender, I'll talk."

Grinning, she pushed the cup away, folding her hands under her chin expectantly.

Drying my cheek, I held back a small smile. Laralie was ridiculous, but maybe I needed this kind of blunt tactic. "You know the guy that sent me that dress?"

Her eyes flashed. "Of course I do. It was gorgeous."

I decided not to tell her what the fate of the dress had been. After getting home and seeing how ruined it was, I'd regretfully tossed it in the trash. "We had a bit of a... fight." There wasn't a better word.

Laralie nodded sagely, not acting surprised. "I figured that was what was going on. Did he do something stupid?"

Opening my mouth, I hesitated. "Maybe."

"Maybe?"

"I don't know. I'm still trying to figure it all out."

At least that part was true.

"I think I get it," she said, sipping at her drink.

"You do?"

"Oh yeah." Her manicured nail jabbed at me. "Turns out he wasn't who you thought he was, huh?"

My eyes flew wide, hands crushing the table edge. She was too close to the reality of it all.

Her hair bounced, her nodding never seeming to stop. "I *knew* he couldn't be that rich. He was faking being a big shot, trying to impress you and all, and you figured it out. Well, good for you, Alexis!"

Laughing sheepishly, I slid deeper in my chair. *Good for me.* "I guess so."

"You're better off without a faker." She blinked at me. "Shit, I just realized something."

My heart thumped. "What?"

Narrowing her eyes, she sighed dramatically. "That dress was probably a fake, too. And here I was, hoping to borrow it from you and never return it again. Life is awful."

Holding my mouth, I bent forward and shook with laughter. The movement rattled me so hard it eased out the tension that had built up for several days. Wiping my eyes, I saw Laralie smiling at me knowingly. "Thanks," I said. "I needed that."

Dropping some money, she stood up. "Don't mention it. Just treat me to a good time in the future and we'll call it even. I haven't been out in forever!"

Together we slid out the restaurant door, the air feeling cleaner to me. My steps were lighter, too. Was the weight that had been sitting on the back of my neck vanishing?

It was a short walk back to our building. With all the people wandering the sidewalks, I didn't notice the detective at first. But he saw me, his arm lifting to wave. "Miss Willow!"

Laralie froze exactly like I did.

He'd been leaning against the stone wall that ran along the sidewalk. Now, he pushed forward, coming our way with determination. I counted his every step until he was right in front of me. "Miss Willow," he said again, tipping his chin. "How are you doing?"

"What do you want?" There was no hiding my sharpness. Roose had left me in pieces when he'd met with me last. I didn't want to repeat that.

It amazed me that he didn't *look* like the threat I felt he was. He didn't even look like he belonged in law enforcement; his hair was too messy, his clothes too casual.

The silence stretched until Laralie broke it. "She asked you a question."

"I'm aware." He hadn't stopped eyeballing me. I wiped my palms on my hips, and he watched that, too. "Miss Willow, I was doing some thinking."

"Were you," I mumbled.

"Yeah. Last time we talked, you were... upset. Part of that seemed to come from your fuzzy memory." Lifting an eyebrow, he pursed his lips. "I'm guessing you haven't remembered anything still?"

I swallowed loudly. "Nothing." Where was he going with this?

Cocking his jaw, Roose sighed. "I'll just jump to it. Miss Willow, I want you to come with me to Old Stone Bank."

I locked my knees out, ignoring how they ached. "I don't... what? Why?"

Laralie lifted her hands, sensing my unease and acting like she was going to catch me if I fell.

"I've done some research. In cases like yours, where a victim—"

Victim. I hated that word, but was he wrong?

"—represses their memories, going back to the scene of the trauma can jolt everything back into place."

Shaking myself head to toe, I breathed in and filled my lower belly. The pressure kept me stable, strong. "No," I said. "I can't go." *Never again. I said I'd never go back.*

"And why is that?" he asked.

I glanced at my building. "We're in a crunch," I lied. "I can't miss any work. I've got to get back before my boss flips out."

Roose's smile ate my confidence away. "Thank goodness I already talked to your boss. He told me he'd be more than happy to let you assist me, in the name of the law and all that. Good guy, that one."

Good guy, alright. I was mentally choking him.

Laralie looked me over, her tone gentle. "Maybe you should go, Alexis."

I leaned away from her. "What?"

"Are your memories from back then really... you know, gone?"

Her concern was throwing me off. The armor I'd crafted out of terror and bitter exhaustion cracked off of me in bits. "Yes," I whispered.

"That would drive me crazy." Her shoulders rode high. "I don't know. As much as this guy is grating my nerves from how up your ass he's being—"

"Excuse me," Roose coughed.

"As much as all that, not knowing would be the worst. If going back there can shake things loose, what's the harm?"

Both the detective and I blinked at her. He was baffled, and I was—amazingly—not as betrayed as I expected to feel. Laralie's heart was in the right place, and she had no idea she was putting me in a tough spot.

Except... maybe she was right. *If it can help me stop blocking things out, isn't it worth the fear?* I wasn't sure, but a sliver of me lit up like a firework at the idea of regaining my memories.

"Alright," I said, trying to mute the defeat in my voice. "I'll see what happens."

How much more could one event ruin my life, anyway?

Laralie reached out, pulling me in for a hug that left me blushing. Then, she backed up the steps, rounding on the detective. "If something bad happens to her," she said flatly, "I'll stick that pen of yours up your ass."

He threw his hands up, managing to look entertained instead of scared. "Why do you keep treating me like I'm the bad guy here?"

She pointed once more, then she waved at me before vanishing inside.

Roose sighed loudly, twisting the pen in his fingers. "She wasn't serious, was she?"

Looking up at him, I lingered on the pen. "You don't want to find out."

His laugh was real, until he saw how I wasn't amused. Coughing, he tucked the pen in his pocket and waved an arm to the left. "Let's get going."

My steps down the sidewalk became heavier and heavier. I had the sense that, in spite of all the promised results, I was heading towards the gallows.

Old Stone bank, the place everything had changed.

No matter how I tried to prepare myself... I didn't know what was waiting for me.

- Chapter Thirteen -

Alexis

The drive went by too fast. It always worked that way when you didn't want to be somewhere, didn't it?

Roose had driven us in an old, beaten up Subaru. Again, I didn't know what I expected from this guy, but it wasn't this. The floor of the car was messy—not with trash, I realized, but crumpled bits of notebook paper.

Nudging one, I tried to read the scribbles, but I was distracted by the sight of a Tool CD underneath. Were detectives allowed to listen to that kind of music? *Good* music?

"Hey," he said, trying to start a conversation for the eighth time. "Thanks again for doing this."

"Thank me if it works." *It won't work.* But what if it did?

In my purse, my phone buzzed. It was loud enough in the silence that Roose glanced at me. "You gonna get that?"

On impulse, I dug inside and peeked at the phone. It had been a text.

Silver: I need to see you.

Clutching the phone, as if the warmth from it was connected to the man himself, I shivered. *If I respond, what do I say?*

Roose coughed politely. "Something come up?"

Nervously, I zipped my purse up. "No no, everything is fine."

"Well, good. Because we're here."

I tasted bile in my mouth. Old Stone Bank was as big as I remembered it. It hadn't changed at all in five years, not that I could see. The pale structure reached for the sky, leaving our car in shadow.

Pain rippled up my forearm; I was crushing my seat unconsciously. Letting it go, I flexed my hand and glanced at Roose. "It's weird," I admitted. "I never planned to come back here."

Leaning in the car door, he watched me with interest. "I wouldn't have asked you to do this if I thought there was another way. You might not believe this, but I don't normally like making girls pissed at me."

I cracked a smile. "That *is* hard to believe."

Warmth entered his eyes. "Listen, Miss Willow... I promise, if it gets to be too much for you, I'll get you out of there."

His sudden kindness threw me for a loop.

He said, "I'm really just trying to put a dangerous man behind bars. "

Dangerous. If I shut my eyes and dug down, I could vaguely recall that the man who'd held me hostage *had* put a gun to my head. Roose had confirmed that last week, too. It was strange that I'd forget such a detail, but I'd done my best to avoid talking or reading about the crime for so long. All of it was a big foggy mess.

Visiting the bank might actually jostle things into place and allow me to remember the past clearly. The idea gave me a sense of dread more than anything.

"Miss Willow?"

Blinking, I said, "Just call me Alexis."

"Alright, Alexis. You can call me Vermont."

Smiling weakly, I nodded. "Okay." I had no plans to call him by his first name.

He smiled back. The moment stretched awkwardly. Finally, he cleared his throat. "Are you going to get out of the car?"

I scurried onto the sidewalk and slammed the door behind me. "Uh, sorry. My mind is all over the place."

He led the way up the large stone steps. I noticed that the closer we got to those giant doors, the closer I stood to the detective. Fear was rustling in my guts, stinging me like a nest of wasps.

Inside, the floors and walls were a rich granite. There were several security guards on the perimeter, and the one nearest to us gave a quick nod. The lack of reaction made me think they recognized the detective.

Stepping to one side, he faced me. "Alright, here we are."

Crossing my arms so hard I was bear-hugging myself, I asked, "Now what?"

His face fell. "Is nothing coming back to you?"

"I guess I remember coming here that day."

"That's it?"

Biting my tongue, I gave him a sour look. Spreading his hands in the air, he said, "Sorry, sorry. I just expected it to all come rushing back to you. Maybe you could try to focus harder," he suggested gingerly. "Walk around. Do you remember where it happened?"

My eyes tracked the room, sliding over the customers, the bank tellers, the shining floors and the velvet ropes. "Not really."

"Let me try and remind you, maybe we have to jump start your memory a bit. It was there." He pointed a thin finger at a spot across the way.

When I looked, I wavered on my feet unsteadily. "I... I guess it *was* over there." The long wall of faces behind computers was giving me vertigo.

Nodding, he motioned for me to follow him. Hesitantly, I did, my knees creaking like old wooden boards in a house. "That's good.

Okay. So you were over here when the robber grabbed you?"

His question was funny. I didn't remember being grabbed at all, so why would I know if it had happened here or... My thoughts trailed away as I looked down at the floor. There was a spot there where the light was hitting just right.

"I remember that," I whispered.

"What?" he asked excitedly.

Ignoring him, I knelt down and touched the hard surface. The light bounced into my eyes, causing me to wrinkle my nose. *Too bright,* I thought. *Just like back then.* Across from me, the walls reflected my image like a mirror. I remembered that, too—how I'd been standing here, watching myself and thinking... What was I thinking?

How cute my dress was. I covered my mouth and gasped into my palm. *That's right.*

I... was here to take out money for my trip out of the city.

For my future.

Colors and images pranced behind my eyes. The memory stabbed into me, fish-hooks that sank into my veins and tugged until everything came tumbling down.

On the fringe of my memories, I started to see something. People... a gun pointed my way... a low, rich voice and firm hands and the realization that everything was ruined and broken and... and...

"Miss Willow?" Roose asked. "Are you— Miss Willow!"

I was already running.

- Chapter Fourteen -

Alexis

I heard Roose calling my name.

I didn't look back.

The fear was real... tangible. It choked me and blurred my eyes. I felt my purse rumbling, knew it had to be the detective calling me over and over.

I can't go back. I won't put myself through that again!

Those memories sickened me, clawing and twisting until I'd been living the terror all over again. The trauma had allowed me to bury it deep. Therapy hadn't even brought it to the surface.

This had come close.

Except I'd stopped it. I'd thrown my hands up over my eyes and insured I couldn't see the ghosts of my past. There was no reason to remember, nothing good could come from it.

I knew just enough about the Old Stone robbery, as much as any other person did or needed to. The sanitized version from the News channel had spelled it out.

Someone had stormed the bank.

They'd held everyone hostage... they'd hacked the systems on site...

And then they'd vanished.

What the hell mattered beyond that?

Why did that day wreck your world? No. Fuck wondering. I didn't need that answer. I just needed to move forward.

I felt like I could run forever.

Bending over at the first crosswalk I came up against, I hung my head and heaved. Great gulps of air filled my lungs. I was so disoriented, it took me a long while to notice my phone was still buzzing.

When it didn't stop, I brushed the sweat from my eyes and grabbed it. *It's Roose,* I told myself, trying to work out an excuse for why I'd fled so suddenly. But the number flashing on my screen wasn't the detective's.

Like I was in a dream, I pushed my thumb on the green icon. "Hello?" I asked.

"Finally," Silver breathed into the device. "Why weren't you picking up?"

All at once, every negative feeling I'd had towards this man washed away. His voice was comforting, even if it sent prickles up my skin. His flat confidence grounded me. He helped melt the terror from my heart.

Shivering, I heard my voice breaking. "Sorry, I was busy."

"What's wrong?" he said quickly. "You sound out of breath."

Hesitating, I backed away from the cross-walk as it blinked with its tiny white signal. "It's nothing. I'm just having a weird day."

"Where are you right now?"

Shit, he sounded really concerned. Again, I reminded myself that I'd been pissed—and confused—because of him. Silver had scared me the other night, and I still didn't know what he'd meant by threatening that I belonged to him. I belonged to *no one*.

But the surety in his tone... it warmed me.

"Pet," he demanded. "Tell me where you are."

"Just down by Heagan street."

"I'm coming to get you."

"What?" I lifted my head, scanning the roads like he'd appear from thin air. "That's not necessary."

"Something is wrong, I can tell. I'm heading there now."

"Just wait a second!" I didn't need him rushing here when I wasn't in any danger. At the same time, fuck, I wanted to look into his eyes all over again. I was itching to touch him... and to get answers.

Not for five years had the world felt more awful than it had minutes ago. Whatever reason I had for distrusting the man who'd been spying on me, he was the only thing that made me feel good.

Was this how drug users justified their choices, too?

I started to turn, and across the street, I glimpsed a building. "Here, listen. There's a coffee shop right across the street, the..." I squinted. "Caffeine. I'll wait inside for you."

"Alright," he said. "I'll be there in fifteen minutes."

The line ended, the click as good as a smack to my head. Was I insane? I wanted to laugh at myself. I'd invited my stalker to have coffee with me. *Maybe he's infected me with that thing—what's it called, Stockholm syndrome?*

232

Ducking across the street, I stood under the cafe's eaves. It was small, the door pink with green edges. Pushing it open, I walked into the comforting warmth. The smell of cinnamon and bread was distracting, and if I needed anything, it was a distraction.

The shop was a cute, tiny little place with low tables and various rugs strewn over the dented hardwoods. Considering the grey-bloated-ready-to-rain weather outside, it was a welcome escape.

Something firm brushed my leg. Unprepared, I jumped sideways, knocking over a shelf of books over. "What the hell?" I gasped.

At my feet, a calico cat flipped its tail and purred.

"Are you alright?" A young woman asked, hurrying over to me, her green apron marking her as an employee. On top of her black, cropped hair, a pair of fluffy white ears perched.

Slowly, I scanned the room again. Then, even slower, I looked up at the chalkboard over on the wall. The name of the shop was scrawled there, and I understood that I'd misread it outside.

It wasn't Caffeine, it was *Caffeline*.

A cat cafe.

Scratching my cheek, I said, "I'm fine, sorry." When I knelt to fix the books, another cat came my way, purring and nudging my thigh.

"It's alright," the cat-eared woman giggled. "The kittens forgive you, so all is well."

Blushing, I straightened the last of the books. Reaching over, I gave the newest cat a quick rub behind its cheek. "I've never been inside this kind of coffee shop before."

"We're new." Waving for me to follow her, the woman said, "My name's Amina. Here, have a seat and when you're ready, just pick from this menu and flag me down."

I sat on top of a big fluffy beanbag, sinking deep in the far corner of the shop. It was pretty busy inside, most chairs occupied by people who chatted or browsed on their laptops. Fingering the menu, I grinned at the tiny drawings of kittens and the funny drink names.

I took it upon myself to order two drinks. Silver shoved through the front door moments after Amina set them in front of me.

He was wearing a midnight blue jacket, open so I could see the black shirt clinging to his torso. *Maybe the cats will attack him, shredding his clothes.* The idea of his sudden nudity made me swallow.

"Pet," he said softly, sitting across from me. His amber irises were burning with a need for answers. "What happened, why aren't you at work?"

I started to answer, then I stopped. "How do you know I was supposed to be working?"

"Do you think I don't keep tabs on where you are?" He chuckled, like *I* was the ridiculous one.

I hid behind my small white cup of green tea. "That's not normal."

"I know."

I'd expected him to act differently, maybe deny right out of the gate that he'd been stalking me. Instead, he was almost proud of it.

He lifted the cup in front of him, sniffing it. "What's this?"

"It's called a Silver Lynx," I said, my cheeks going pinker. "I thought you'd appreciate the name."

Grinning, he watched me intently. "I do." His sip was slow, lingering. When he finished, he breathed out. "We should talk."

"About the other night? Yeah. I think we should, too." My tongue pressed each word like a hammer on an anvil, giving them all a blade's edge. "I need to know how long you've been following me."

"You're very demanding for a pet."

"I'm *not* your pet."

"You are." Glancing down, he motioned at a black cat that was stretched out on the cafe floor. It flicked its ears, miraculously swaying over so Silver could rub its head. "You're not wearing a leash anyone can see, but it's there." When he shot his stare back to me, I stiffened. "And I'm holding the other end of it."

Bunching up my shoulders, I sighed. "Tell me how you know me."

"Tell me what had you so flustered earlier."

I came close to arguing with him. Really, though, I was too burnt out to find the energy. *If I give him answers, he might finally give me some.* Hanging my head, I glanced at the nearby wall. "There's a detective that's been following me as much as *you* have." I frowned at him. "He's been trying to grill me for information."

Silver sat up so quickly that the cat jumped away. "Detective?"

"It's stupid." Shaking my head, I peered through my eyelashes at him. "I feel weird explaining it, even."

"Don't, just take your time," he said gently.

He switches from domineering to kind like a flip of a light switch. In spite of my observation, the sudden warmth inside of me wasn't just from my tea. "Alright. Well, this guy —Detective Roose—he thinks I can help him with an old case. Except, I don't think I can. I kind of don't remember much about what happened, and it was so long ago, you know?"

238

Silver considered me, his hands resting lightly on the table. "I see. He wants your help, even though you can't remember the details he needs? Why can't you remember, amnesia?"

My laugh was nervous. "Amnesia is too intense a word for it. I can recall bits and pieces, if I try." *I don't want to try.* "He thought he had a way to fix it so I'd remember more clearly. Earlier, he took me back to where it all happened—the crime, I mean. Guess he wanted the location to jog my memory."

"And it didn't."

"No," I agreed. "It didn't."

Smoothing his shirt, he said, "So that's why you were so distraught on the phone. You couldn't remember anything, even after he forced you."

"I wouldn't say forced." Swirling my spoon on my tea, I watched my reflection ripple. "Or maybe it *was* forced. Either way, it was a waste of time."

"These kind of things should be handled more gingerly."

Lifting my chin, I studied him. He seemed so relaxed, but I sensed he was as coiled as the cats were. "If you've forgotten things, it's for a reason. Trying to break that vault open before your psyche is ready could damage you."

The way he gave me an excuse for burying my past so firmly, it made me grateful. So grateful, that I almost forgot he hadn't answered any of *my* questions, still. "Hey," I said sharply. "It's your turn. Tell me when you began stalking me, and why!"

"Knowing where you work isn't really stalking."

"It is! And you knew where my post office was, where I live... you know a *lot*, Silver. Why?"

"Because I want to know everything about you."

Turning crimson, I let my hands fall down to my lap. "That's not enough. I need more."

"So do I."

"Stop that!" I blurted. I grabbed for some control, hating how he was turning things around on me. "Tell me what happened the other night, why were you acting so weird?"

"You mean why was I reveling in how I'd conquered your body? How I'd turned you into my play thing, and how I made it clear you belong to me?"

This wasn't the inquisition I'd expected. The more we talked, the more I found my anger mutating into something just as hot, but entirely different.

I squinted at my knees, unable to speak. I was furious at his slippery answers, and fumbling with the blunt honestly he kept throwing at me. Hadn't I run away from him three nights ago? At what point had I stopped feeling afraid of this man?

Silver tapped the table, making me look up. "I know that I was intimidating. I couldn't help it, Pet. I was relishing in the pure *sensation* of power that being with you gave me. Nothing could have been better than that moment. I never wanted it to end."

My heart was one big flickering ball of excitement. "I didn't either," I whispered softly.

Under the table, his fingers found my knee, grazing it. My pulse fluttered quicker. "I have something for you."

"What is it?"

"Well..." Reaching into his pocket, he bent forward. I had the sudden idea he was about to get down on one knee.

"Silver," I gasped, covering my mouth. "What are you doing?"

He grinned, sliding a set of keys into the light. "Here, take these."

The sight of them calmed my heart. I wasn't ready for a damn proposal, but at the same time, I endured a stab of disappointment. Reaching out, I stopped inches from taking them. "Are those your house keys?"

He dropped them so that I had no choice but to catch them. "More than that. There's a key there for everything I own. I'm an open book to you, Pet."

"I... why?" Clutching them, I enjoyed how they still held his warmth.

"Because I want to make it possible for you to reach me at any time. I never want you to feel like I'm not there for you. No lock can keep us apart."

The last remnant of my uncertainty faded into the background. It was still there, but buried under the heavy waves of my own surprise. "This might be the most valuable gift you've given me," I whispered, tucking the keys in my purse.

"Speaking of gifts," he said, sipping at his tea, "When you were throwing mine away, which ones ended up in the trash?"

Linking my fingers, I bit my lip guiltily. I didn't want to be reminded of how I'd thrown all those boxes into a dumpster. "I don't know, I chucked out a bunch of stuff that I never even opened."

"You saw none of it?"

Oh no, I thought. *I did see one thing in particular. I even wore it.* I'd never tell him that part. "I kind of threw away some really fancy lingerie." That memory wasn't a pleasant one.

"That's perfect."

I sat there for a moment, digesting his response. "I'm sorry, what?"

Silver's hand vanished from my leg. He rose, his open palm waiting expectantly for mine. "You've given us something to do for the afternoon."

I didn't know what he was talking about.

I had no clue why Silver was following me, why he was using a fake name, or what his plans for us—for me—even were.

When my fingers slid into his, we both squeezed.

- Chapter Fifteen -

Alexis

His car keys jingled as he handed them over to the valet. I was still sitting in the Mustang, the windows blocking me from hearing their voices. Silver was smiling, talking with the other man as he handed over some cash.

It made me thrill to have Silver open the passenger door. He tugged me free, then captured me all over again when we swayed close. Our chests nearly touched, but I gasped like we'd slammed together.

It was obvious from how he lingered, fingers clutching mine, that he was battling with wrapping me in his arms and kissing me right in front of the gathered valets. He stepped back, fingers tucking into his jeans like he had to put them somewhere before he lost control and snatched me up all over again.

Motioning with his sharp jaw, he said, "Come on, let's go inside."

The moment we stepped through the glass doors and into the lingerie shop, I wished I'd dressed nicer. My plan for the day had been to stumble through work without falling apart. Maybe I'd order Chinese and watch something late into the night.

Those plans don't require fancy clothes, so all I'd put on was plain black pants and a loose beige sweater.

Standing under the crystal decorations and the golden lights, I felt like a fraud. Mannequins shaped like impossibly perfect people cocked their hips all over the room. They were wearing lace, leather, satin... every fabric I could have named, and many I couldn't.

"How may I help you?" The woman who approached was draped in a black skirt and a crisp blouse. Her hands glinted with jewels, while her teeth sparkled even more so.

Silver gave me a nudge. "We're looking for a few different sets, whatever your finest quality items are."

"Oh no," I said, glancing between them. "Just one set, and it doesn't have to be *that* fine."

"It does." He nodded knowingly at the woman. "Use your best judgment."

"Really," I said. "Don't listen to him."

"I think she'll be happy to listen to me. Just like you should be, *Pet.*"

That shut me up; I couldn't believe he'd called me that name in front of a stranger. The woman—whose name was Donna, according to her tag—gave us both a long stare. I was amazed she was still smiling when she spoke. "Follow me, Miss. I think I can make you both happy."

Glaring sideways at Silver, I mouthed, "*Stop it.*"

He just smirked even brighter.

Donna guided me through the tunnels of clothing and away from Silver. "Do you have a favorite color?"

Grazing my eyes over the lingerie, I hummed. "Green is nice, but so is purple."

Snatching a few things off the racks, she smiled at me. "Honestly? I think white suits you better." Then, like she was considering her own comment, she stood on her toes and looked behind me. I followed her eyes, noticing she was making sure Silver was out of earshot. "Is he your Dom?"

"My *what?*"

"Dom." She said it so matter of fact. "Masters, whatever you want to call them. Guys who like to pretend they can control their women."

My mouth gaped, no sound escaping.

Donna covered her own mouth in horror. "Oh gosh, I didn't mean that to sound bad. I've got nothing against the whole submissive sex slave kind of thing, I swear! I've even got a friend who looks for that on Tinder."

I gestured with my hands between us, punctuating each word. "*It's not like that.*"

She hoisted the pile of lingerie onto her shoulder. "But he called you his pet."

"That—that's just a nickname he has for me!" I laughed too loudly. "Like a *pet* name, get it? Do you get it?" My eyebrows lowered. "Tell me you get it."

"I get it, I get it!" Her heels snapped over the floor, taking us through a curtain. Inside, there were a few stalls and a single mirrored wall. "Here, try these on. If you need anything, call for me."

"Right. I will." When she ducked through the curtain, I slumped sideways with a groan. Had she really called Silver my master?

Even if he could control my excitement, control my breathing... my heart... or how fast or slow I climaxed...

He wasn't my fucking master.

Moving into a stall, I shut the door. Donna had left me way too much to try on. I wasn't going to bother with all of it, honestly.

Picking through the stack, I brushed an ivory corset covered in black lace. The pattern looked like leaves that were spiraling in an autumn breeze. I was reminded of the day I'd slid into the outfit Silver had sent.

Back then, he'd been known as *S* to me. A figment, a phantom... a stranger. But even so, I'd dressed in that lingerie with glee.

Trembling, I started to breathe faster. Stripping out of my clothes, I hooked the corset into place. It forced my breasts up, cupping them and creating cleavage like I'd never had. The panties were boy-cut, almost slippery to the touch.

When I bent down to grab at the thigh-highs Donna had left to match, a small sound hit my ears. I'd barely straightened up when the door to my private box cracked open. Silver leaned inside, his eyes eating me up in one quick swoop. "Fucking hell," he breathed out.

"What are you doing?" I gasped, backing up; there was no where to run. "I've barely tried anything on yet. You should wait outside."

He closed the door, the lock clicking sharply. Advancing on me, his nostrils flared. "How could I wait when I knew you were stripping in here?" His eyes swept over me. "You're so fucking beautiful. I can't handle it."

"Silver," I started to say.

His hands came down hard on the wall behind me, boxing me in. I felt the structure shake, my knees copying the motion. "I need you right now. Right here."

I lifted my fingers, but he just linked them with his and shoved my wrists on the

252

wall. I couldn't argue, he'd stolen my voice—
and he was stealing my strength.

Silver's hands raked down the corset, his
mouth tackling mine. Wet, warm lips dulled my
senses. My whimper weaved through the cotton
in my brain, so soft it could have been a dream.

Reaching between my thighs, he stroked
the outside of my silken panties. I clenched
around him, trying to push him away. All I did
was hold him closer. I was an accomplice in my
own capture.

"We can't, we really can't!"

"I'm not letting you talk me out of this.
Not when I can smell how turned on you are
from here." His thumb rubbed along my slit,
fondling my pussy up and down. Any chance I
had of denying him the truth—that he was
ruining the panties we hadn't bought yet—
faded under my own soft moans.

"Excuse me!" The heavy thudding of an
angry fist assaulted the door. "I can hear you

two in there!" Donna shouted. "Stop that this instant, or I'm calling security!"

Silver pulled away from me. I was cold from panic, but he was smiling like this was a game. Everything was, to him. "Stay here," he said. Digging into his jacket, he slid out his wallet and thumbed through the cash.

He was carrying several thousand fucking dollars.

Turning, he unlocked the stall. I glimpsed Donna, her face furiously beet red. I was sure that she thought the worst of me. Every claim I'd made earlier about how Silver and I weren't playing at being master and slave had been snuffed out.

"Sir," she started to say.

Silver cut her off, his hand fanning out some bills. "Take this and leave us alone."

Her eyes bugged out, dancing between the money and his grin. "I—what?"

"And this," he went on, sliding another thick stack her way. "Is for the lingerie. We'll be taking everything."

Donna had gone silent, but her hungry stare said plenty. Taking the money, she shot me one quick look...

And then she shut the door for us.

Silver spun, the centers of his eyes glowing. "Now, where were we?"

Pulling his pants down slightly, he shoved me back on the wall. His arms tangled around me, my hair blinding me. Some got in my mouth when I kissed him, but neither of us cared.

"Feel me," he demanded, guiding my palm between us. The heat of his straining cock through his underwear was maddening. He controlled me, grinding my skin against him.

"Are we really doing this?" I asked softly. I was distracted by how good his length felt in my hand.

Spinning me, he grabbed my hair and bent my chest into the wall. I wouldn't have moved, but his palm came down—crispy spanking my ass. "Hey!" I gasped, trying to face him. He held tighter, slapping my other cheek.

"I want the store to hear you," he said, brushing his suddenly exposed cock over my lower back. "Make some noise, Pet. Let them know how good you're getting fucked."

Biting my own wrist, I shook my head. My body was furiously turned on, but emotionally, I wasn't ready to tell that to the world.

The sound of paper ripping announced the condom. The new panties were guided down, still hugging around my hips. Slick from my juice, he rubbed his dick between my ass cheeks. I tensed up, peering back at him. "Not there."

"No?" he asked, grinning.

"I can't. I haven't... and not like this."

256

"Relax." Licking his thumb lewdly, he brought it near my asshole. When I jumped, his eyes got sharper. "I love when you squirm. I'm not going to fuck your ass, Pet. Not now, anyway."

Squeezing my hips, he hooked my panties and moved them aside. With the fabric cutting into both of us, he fed his cock into me. Groaning, I forgot where we were. I was too hungry for release, a slave to my own passion.

This bastard was right.

He could control me.

Silver fucked me with full, hard strokes. There was no patience. I had the feeling that he'd been lusting for me since we'd first had sex. He'd had a taste, and being forced to wait for more had cracked some of his stoniness.

"Yes," he growled, hunching over me. "Fuck, yes. Drive your pussy back onto me. Do it!"

I obeyed, already gyrating helplessly.

A wave made of butter and trembles skipped down to my clit. My muscles clenched, making his every movement delicious. I was coming before I sensed it, caught off guard and openly whimpering.

It must have set him off; he clung to me, hammering into my twitching pussy. I thought, when his release tipped over, that he sighed in content. But that was a noise too soft for a man like him.

I must have imagined it.

Sliding backwards, he traced his fingers through my hair. "I missed you."

Stunned, I remained where I was against the wall. He turned away, zipping his pants, effectively stopping me from responding.

I missed you, too, was my unsaid answer.

Gathering up the lingerie, he smiled at me over his shoulder. "Let's get out of here before they call security on us."

"But you paid that woman to leave us alone."

"Money doesn't guarantee people will act as you expect."

Unsure what he was talking about, I changed into my old clothes, grabbed up the ones we'd soiled, and followed him out of the stall.

Everyone in the store looked at me when I appeared. They'd heard everything.

I kept my head down all the way until we got in his car.

****

"Listen," I said, staring out the window at the world as it rolled by. "Back there, the woman at the store... she called you a Dom. Was she right?"

Silver was quiet for so long that I gave in and glanced at him. He was facing the road, focused—thoughtful. "No," he said, stretching the word out. "I'm not."

Shifting, I faced him fully. "Then what is all this? Calling me your pet and stuff."

The centers of his dark eyes flicked at me, then away. "It's just how I feel."

Pursing my lips, I willed him to explain further. He didn't. "You *feel* like I'm your pet? That makes no sense."

His smile was absent. "I guess so."

"That's all you have to say?"

"What more is there?"

Sinking into my seat, I breathed in sharply. "Any kind of explanation would do."

He went quiet again. Tapping my knee in frustration, I opened my mouth, but he spoke first. "I don't think it's possible to explain how I feel. Some things don't work like that. If they did—" It was like he caught himself, his teeth cutting together to end his thoughts.

I'd been so fixated on him that I didn't notice our surroundings. Not until he started to slow down around a curve. We'd pulled into a wide open field. I could see everything for miles, so the planes were easy to spot.

"This is..." Blinking, I swung around to press my hands on my window. "An airport?"

"A private airfield."

His car rolled to a halt in the middle of the concrete. In front of us waited a small jet, the wings shining gold and red in spite of the cloud cover. He turned the engine off, and I felt him staring at me.

I said, "That's yours, isn't it?"

"Of course."

Sitting back, I looked over my shoulder at him. His expression was neutral. "Silver, why are we here?"

He didn't smile, but I kept expecting him too. "I need some sun, and there's no better place for sun in February than LA."

My mouth fell open. "You want to fly to Los Angeles?" My brain tickled with understanding. "You want both of us to go, don't you?"

"It'd be good to get away, just for the weekend."

My eyes spun back to the jet in wonder. "I thought you said we were going to spend the *afternoon* together?"

"You don't want to go?" His voice was full of that soft, velvet quality unique to him.

I couldn't stop staring at the jet. It was as foreign to me as a damn unicorn. It had been years since I'd flown.

Since I'd left this city.

I whispered, "I always wanted to visit LA."

"Why didn't you?"

There was a level of seriousness in how he asked that. I was tempted to tell him the truth; that I'd been fucked up by a traumatic event that had thrown my whole life out of orbit.

I didn't have the heart to ruin the moment.

Flicking my fingers, I erased his question. "Things just got in the way." *What's in the way now?*

"What are you doing?" he asked, seeing me pull out my phone.

My thumb moved over the keys. I was acting fast, trying to keep ahead of my nerves so they wouldn't stop me in my tracks. "I'm letting my mom know I'll be in LA for the weekend. Where are we going to be staying?"

He grinned slyly. "You're telling your mom where you'll be? Are you worried I'll do something to you out there?"

Sending the text, I gave him a pointed look. "Exactly. The address, please."

Suddenly, my phone vibrated. My mother was calling me. We both watched as I ended the call before it came through.

He said, "I thought you were telling her our plans."

"Texting is one thing, but this..."

"You don't want to talk to her over the phone?"

"Do *you* want to explain to her what the hell we're doing?" *What are we doing? What am I doing?* "Because I'd rather not get into that conversation."

My phone buzzed again.

I groaned, palming my face. "Maybe I shouldn't have told her, now she won't leave me alone."

He plucked the phone from my fingers before I could react. "Hello?" he asked. The smirk he sent me went ear to ear.

Clutching at my chest, I sputtered. "W—you—oh fuck. Oh fuck oh fuck, *hang up the phone.*"

"Yes, Alexis is here," he said, leaning back in his seat. "But she had to run to the restroom." He was relaxed, his voice thick and gentle. "Who am I? I'm her boyfriend, Silver."

My tongue felt like it was shrinking.

"It *is* a strange name, I know." He winked at me, then went quiet as he listened. "Oh, we've been dating some time. I'm sure she had her reasons for not telling you."

Shiiiiiit.

He sat up, and I could hear the rising tone of my mom. I thought she had to be angry, and I was working on how to back out of this whole mess.

"Yes," he chuckled. "I'll be sure to tell her that when she gets back. Our waiter is coming with the check, here he is, I have to go.

Yes, sorry. You have a good night too, Miss Willow." He hung up, tossing me my phone.

I didn't catch it; it just bounced off my knee and hit the floor. "What did she say?"

"You look like you're going to be sick." Leaning my way, he brushed my neck. "I can feel your pulse going wild."

"What did she say?"

Laughing, he nuzzled my cheek and kissed my ear. "She was relieved to hear you were *finally* dating someone. She insisted I show you a good time in LA. Your mom is very nice, Pet."

Pushing my hands against his jaw, I forced him an inch away from me. My emotions bubbled together in a vat, I couldn't tell one from the other. In retrospect, it made sense that my mother would be happy for me. She'd been pushing me to meet people forever.

But keeping Silver a secret wasn't just for her. I didn't want *anyone* to know that I

266

was falling for a man that was more questions than answers. He'd been *stalking* me, how did I tell people how we met?

Just imagining that conversation was giving me hives. The instant the world cracked the shell around us and saw what we were becoming... what *I* was becoming...

I'd have to admit it.

Was I ready for that?

In the window over his shoulder, I saw I was smiling. I hadn't felt my lips making the shape, but now, the sensation of joy slid into the rest of me. Pushing my mouth to his, I rolled my tongue over his teeth.

The animal-sound he made set my nerves on fire.

Just as quick, I pushed him away. He was breathing hard, coiled and ready to spring back on top of me. "What are you waiting for?" I asked. "You're supposed to show me a good time in LA. Get to it."

His rich eyes were glowing. I half expected him to ignore my request. Brushing his hair back, he straightened his jacket and smiled. "I'm going to blow your world apart this weekend. When we get back to this city, you won't be the same."

And I laughed, and I smiled, because in that moment I was *happy*.

If only I'd known how right he would be.

- Chapter Sixteen -
Alexis

The jet was, quite possibly, the most luxurious thing I'd ever been inside of. We were the only occupants, minus the pilot. When I'd met him, he'd grinned so wide I'd seen his fake gold tooth.

The interior of the jet was creamy caramel. I wriggled into the heated seat, stretched it all the way out, and then looked at Silver in amazement. "How do you do it?"

"How do I do what?" he asked, sitting next to me.

"Not just fly around in this thing all the time?"

Laughing, he poured himself a drink from the small bar that was set securely into the wall. "I'm rich, but fuel isn't free."

Nodding sagely, I accepted the glass he offered me. When he raised his, I copied him. "What are we toasting to?" I asked.

"How about... to good times, future adventures, and two whole nights away to ourselves."

That last part was said with slow, deliberate words. I blushed, clinking my glass on his. "That sounds wonderful."

It was a smooth flight. In fact, the only thing that startled me was when Silver's phone rang while we were high in the clouds. It scared me so hard that I dropped my water bottle. "You get reception up here?" I asked. Then, more importantly, "Won't that crash the plane?"

Silver leveled a doubtful look on me. "Yes. We're definitely going to crash."

When he didn't start panicking, I gave him a shove. He turned it around, pulling me close and kissing my neck. He whispered, "I'd never let anything happen to you, Pet."

His promise made me dizzy.

Untangling from me, he waved his phone. "Give me one minute, it's work."

It had been too easy to forget that he had any responsibilities beyond lavishing me with his time and his money. But of course he had to work, and I was glad he couldn't tell how ashamed I was to have forgotten that.

"Hello?" he said, shifting to face the window. "I'm in the middle of something." Silver went quiet, his eyes narrowing a hair as he listened. "Yes, I know the spare key is gone." He glanced at me. "Florian, I'm going to be gone all weekend. You don't need to get into my office, just send them the design notes on Monday."

His office? Hugging my purse close, I listened to the muffle jingle inside. *Did he actually give me a key to his workplace?*

Digging his fingers into his scalp, Silver bit out his next sentence. "I don't fucking care. I'm not turning around. I'll be back Monday, understand? Or do you want me to email that to you, too?" He shut his eyes, breathing out. "That's what I thought. Bye."

I waited until he'd put the phone away, but his eyes were still closed. "Is everything okay?"

Silver blinked at me, like he'd forgotten I was there. "It's fine." Circling me with his arm, he guided me into his lap. "It's even better, now."

****

Walking through LAX, I gazed at the giant airport in wonder. It was insanely busy, people shoving here and there while we headed towards the exit. As we were passing one of the millions of gift shops, I slowed down.

Hanging on racks were a few generic "I Heart LA" sweaters.

"Did you want a souvenir?" he asked.

"Oh, no, it's fine."

He studied my face, then turned towards the woman behind the kiosk. "We'll take one of those."

She nodded quickly, jumping up to grab for them. "Pink or blue?" she asked.

I'd gone silent, marveling at Silver's quick decision to buy me one of the sweaters. They both waited on me, so I cleared my throat. "Pink is fine."

She handed it over, taking Silver's cash. It was soft and thick, better quality than I expected, considering it was an airport sweater. "Do you like it?" he asked.

Smiling, I hugged it tight. "Call me cheesy, but I kind of do."

"Put it on."

"What, right now?"

His eyes glinted, and I thought he couldn't have been more serious. Chewing the side of my mouth, I pulled it over my head, messing up my hair.

Tilting his head, he peered at me. "How do you look amazing in everything you put on?"

"Stop it," I said, blushing hotter. I saw myself in a window, and I wondered what *he* was seeing, because I just looked like I'd flown for several hours and needed some caffeine.

His fingers slid into mine, holding tight. "Come on, let's get to my place."

Sinking into the sensation of his touch, I followed at his side.

The taxi ride was smooth, and while I boggled out the window at the palm trees and buildings, Silver never let go of my hand. Once, he pulled me close, kissing me without a care that our driver was watching.

He held on all the way until we pulled up outside of a bright white condo, and it was only

274

because he needed both hands to gather his suitcase and the shopping bag we'd brought from the lingerie store.

"This is gorgeous," I said, once we'd arrived on his floor. I spun so I could see every angle; it was even bigger than the place he had in Portland. It also looked more modern, everything sort of minimized—the chairs, the glass tables, the ceramic bar.

"I'm glad you like it. I haven't been back for a month, it's good to see everything is still here." His chuckle said he didn't really expect someone would rob him. And, considering the security in the lobby, why would he?

"Want a drink before we go out?"

"Just where are we going?" I asked, stopping to squint at him. "I didn't bring much to wear besides all that lingerie."

I'd meant it as a joke, but his sharp smirk made me pause. "You *could* wear one of those outfits and get away with it. But I've got something on hand that will work."

"'On hand?'" I repeated. Silver headed to one side of the giant room, crossing the wide window view of LA that some people would kill for. Kneeling by the suitcase he'd packed in his car, he dug inside.

In a flash of fabric, he yanked a black dress into view.

Covering my mouth, I swayed close enough to see the outfit. "Why do you have that?"

"It doesn't matter." He stood, offering it to me.

In wonderment, I ran my fingers over the the dress, but I didn't take it. "It *does* matter. When did you pack this?"

He said, "When I decided last night that I'd convince you to come to LA with me."

Amazed, I started to close my grip on the black dress's hem—then I stopped. "We're not going to a funeral, are we?"

Cracking a smile, he shrugged. "If we were, you'd look incredibly stunning."

"I'm sure the grieving family would appreciate that," I teased. Gently, I looped it over my arms. "Okay, so I've got a dress. What about—"

"Shoes?" He nodded downwards, and I followed his eyes to spot a pair of glossy heels in the bottom of the suitcase.

Just how far ahead had he planned our evening?

Is he planning beyond that? I suddenly wondered.

Shaking myself, I grabbed the shoes and cradled everything in my arms. "I guess I'll get ready for... whatever you've got in mind."

He smiled so hard that his eyes crinkled on the edges.

****

I'd never seen anything like Hollywood at night.

It was everything I'd ever dreamed of.

"You're going to fall out the window," Silver said, chuckling.

He was driving a convertible—another car he owned that stayed in LA—and I'd insisted the top stay down. My hair was tangling over my face, but with the taste of the wild night life on my tongue, I didn't care.

Silver pulled down an alley, parking on a quiet street. We were surrounded by graffiti and the air lost its exciting energy, replaced by garbage. Even so, I noticed many of the other cars in front of meters were as expensive as Silver's.

Taking my arm, he helped me down the sloped sidewalk. There was no line in front of the barely lit entrance. A man who looked weirdly like the man who'd checked my name off at the Red and Ripe sat in a rusted chair.

With a quick glance at Silver, he nodded for us to go inside. I'd expected him to ask our names, but maybe he didn't need to. Or maybe he knew who Silver was? Eyeing him, I was blinded by darkness as we passed through a hallway.

"Are you ready?" he asked, pulling up short in front of a black door.

Laughing, I looped my arm with his. "Do you honestly expect me to turn back now?"

Winking, he let me inside.

Hanging from the ceiling were giant cages. Gold and opal, they shimmered under the circles of lights overhead. That was majestic enough, but it was the contents of the cages that took my breath away.

Women. Real, actual live women. Flashes of color highlighted their nudity, white boots the only things they wore. Each of them swung and gyrated, and a few weren't alone behind their bars.

I had a clear shot of a man fucking one of the dancer's doggy-style.

"Well?" Silver asked, running his fingers up my spine. "Is this okay?"

My heart was rumbling, but I managed to meet his stare. "This is what you planned for tonight?"

There was no hint of shame in his face. "Last time, our fun was cut short."

Anxiousness crept into my bones. It made a home there, refusing to be evicted no matter how I tried to calm myself.

Around us, club-goers danced and shouted. They wore everything from suits to barely-there jean shorts. I didn't know the name of this place, but it only seemed to care about one thing; being erotic.

Silver urged me further into the swaying bodies, his touch as firm as any chain. Turning me in a circle, he brought me close to one of the large, white cushions set around the outside of the club's dance floor. This was good, because my legs were wobbling on my heels; I needed to sit.

"Can I get you a drink?" he asked, looming over me when I settled.

"That'd be great." Laughing uneasily, I grabbed his sleeve before he could leave. His eyebrows went up. "Look, I know I seem nervous. Okay, I *am* nervous. But it's okay, I'm not going to run away this time."

Silver considered me carefully. There was a softness in his eyes, just beyond that ever-constant layer of mystery. "I believe you. So let me go get you that drink."

My hand fell away. I set it in my lap once he'd slipped out of view among the throngs of people. Crossing my bare legs, I looked around and tried to act normal. *What's normal for a sex club?* Jeez, if Laralie knew I'd come to one of these places—twice, even—she'd lose her mind.

Silver broke back into my eyesight, two glasses in his hands. He was smiling, but right as he got close to me, his attention swept just over my shoulder... and his joy vanished.

"Hey! Kes!" Someone was waving an arm, heading our way with purpose. The man looked as if someone had poured a hundred pounds of nails into a smelter, then carved the hard metal into a multitude of swords.

I'd never seen someone with such fierce features. When he swung out a hand to shake Silver's, I nearly reached out to stop him, just in case he'd slice the other man's arm in two.

Kes, as in Keswick? I knew that name from Silver's business card. A quick peek at him showed me the tension in his face. Was he wondering if I'd heard, or what I was thinking?

I played dumb, taking the drink from Silver. "Gerard," he said, reaching out to join the handshake. "I haven't seen you in some time."

"Over a year, at least," the stranger laughed. Gerard glanced between us, his lips coiling on the corners. "And who is this lovely lady?"

Sipping my drink, I looked at the other man curiously. How did he know Silver? "I'm Alexis," I said, waving briefly.

Gerard gave Silver a thoughtful look. I tried to read it, but I failed. "Well," he said, gesturing around. "I never imagined I'd see you back in California. Didn't you move to Portland?"

"I still do some business here," he said.

"Yeah?" Gerard cocked his head. "What about Florian, he here too? Man, everyone was upset when you guys bailed."

"It's not bailing to take what you know and make something for yourself."

Gerard was watching me from the corner of his eye. Silver was, too. "I remember you guys leaving even after I offered you a severe salary increase. Guess you were too good to work for anyone else, huh?" He flashed an insincere grin.

This is awkward. I hadn't thought I'd get caught in a subtle war like this. My drink was half gone, I saw Silver hadn't touched his.

Gerard pointed his too-sharp chin at me. "Alexis, right?" He paused, his tongue running over his lips. "You been to this club before?"

"Oh, uh, no." I smiled apologetically.

Next to me, Silver stiffened and said, "That's enough."

He leaned close, watching Silver as he spoke to me. "You do know what happens here, though?"

"Gerard."

284

"If not, I'm sure he can show you around," the man went on. "He's been here a lot. Shown plenty of others what to expect, if you get me."

He's pissing Silver off by making me uncomfortable. Silver and Gerard had definitely parted on bad terms. He was trying to make me a casualty. I had other ideas.

Silver stepped forward, his knuckles tensing around his glass. Gerard was watching him with a delighted smirk. That meant he didn't see me when I stood tall, my arm pulling back.

"Hey!" Gerard gasped, jumping as the last of my drink soaked his face and shirt.

Setting the glass down, I hooked my arm on Silver's. "You're right," I said, smiling sweetly. "He *can* show me how this place works. Thanks." With a firm pull, I led Silver into the crowd.

I was acting calm, but my pulse was racing. Silver yanked me sideways, his fingers on my shoulders while he stared at my face. Amazingly, his look of shock erased my nerves —I started laughing.

He said, "You threw your drink on him."

"Yeah," I said. "I did. He was being an ass."

Silver pulled me into a rough hug. Knowing that I'd made him happy was an aphrodisiac. It must have been for him, too, because he held me around my hips and guided me to a wall. His palms cupped my ass through my dress, mauling me as he breathed on my neck.

We were grinding together, the music only partially creating our tempo; we had a beat all our own. He hovered above me, his hands touching me all over like he had a million fingers. Tracing down the small of my back, he crossed over my hip—my thigh.

Silver froze, his eyes glinting in the blue club lights. Bending in, he spoke into my ear. "Are you wearing some of the lingerie?"

Pushing off my heels, I kissed the corner of his jaw. "Why don't you find out?"

His mouth twitched, his expression shifting. He was asking me a question with his silence. *Are you sure?* Silver was checking in to see if I was willing to play here.

When we'd first met, I'd been terrified of the concept. I'd seen the people having sex in public and I'd backed down instantly. I'd been so scared.

Now, I wasn't.

His hips thrust, pinning me to the wall. I felt eyes on us instantly, even if I was too busy kissing him to see. The world was a tornado of colors and sound, but it all centered here—right here—with this man.

Coiling his fist in my hair, he wrenched my head back. Teeth found my throat, my ear...

287

and then they vanished. Panting, I gazed up at him with impatience. He held me steady, not letting me do much more than wriggle. Silver was so damn good at teasing me. "Please," I hissed, willing him to go further with just my eyes.

And then I felt the shift in his mood.

Silver was breathing heavy, his teeth close to snarling. To anyone else, he was a creature on the verge of leaping forward to consume anything in his path. He'd stopped himself, but not because he was trying to drive me wild.

"What's wrong?" I asked, blinking up at him.

There was turmoil in his roiling stare. If I looked long enough, I thought I'd understand him better—who he was, what motivated him, everything.

Silver cupped my cheeks, then he grabbed my arm and pulled me away from the wall. "Not here," he said over the din of music. "I—not here. I can't here, not anymore."

Not anymore?

"Wait!" I said, pulling on him to slow his retreat. "I don't understand! Did I do something wrong? I'm okay with it! Really! I wasn't before, but now I—"

"*I'm* not okay with it!" He growled, whirling on me. Fuck, he looked so confused and angry. I must have flinched, because he pulled up short, clutching for my hands. "It's not you," he said, strain in his voice. "It's—I just can't. For some fucking reason I can't handle the idea of anyone else... anyone *ever* seeing you like that. Just me." His eyes went hot. "Only me."

Heat pushed at the back of my throat. It kept going, I quickly rubbed at my face to stop the overwhelming tears. "Idiot," I said, my smile cracking. "You're going to make me cry over not fucking me in a sex club. How can you do that to me, huh?"

He pulled me to his side and kissed my temple. The sweetness went out of him, his hard fingertips searching between my thighs. "Let's get out of here before I change my mind. I need you right now."

Shivering, I let him guide me through the crowd. "Waiting till we get back to your place will be hard."

"My place?" He chuckled, glancing at me. His hand squeezed. "We're not going that far."

"Then where...?" We stumbled past the security guard. The alley air was cool, welcome on my searing skin. I knew what he was planning, just seconds before he ripped his car door open and shoved me inside the backseat. My ass slipped on the smooth leather.

The door slammed behind him. "Let me eat your pussy," he growled. "I need to taste you. I've never been so fucking hard, Pet. I'm going to bury my face between your thighs until one of us passes out."

My eyes fluttered, pleasure weakening my muscles. It was easy for him to spread my legs, driving me further into the seat. Then he hiked my dress up, freezing at the sight of my soaked panties. When he bent close, tugging them off with his teeth, I realized he might be serious about promising to eat me out until one of us was unconscious.

"Hold on," I said, pawing at his hair. "I want to go back to your place."

"No. I can't hold off that long."

"You don't have to." Sitting up, I climbed into the passenger seat. He gave me a curious look, so I leaned over to the driver's side and made a lewd motion.

Laughing, he hooked his arm over the back of the seat. "Road head?"

Flushing, my eyes sparkled with my excitement. "Is that the name? I've never done it."

"You've given blow jobs, though?"

"I—yeah."

"Do you promise not to bite?"

I blinked in horror. "I'd never!"

Smirking, he tugged me towards him by my hair. "Good girl. Then move over."

I scooted out of the way so he could climb into the driver's seat. When he looked at me expectantly, I inched forward into his lap, my hands on his thighs. The sensation of his palm on my scalp tweaked my senses into overdrive.

He turned the key, and I yanked down his jeans.

Silver rocked in his seat, growling and vibrating with need. Gripping the base of his cock, I suckled the tip carefully.

It was a wonder we made it back to his place in one piece.

- Chapter Seventeen -
Silver

She peeled the dress over her head, standing against the wall. I sat up on the bed, my cock bouncing like it was nodding along with me. "You're the fucking sexist woman I've ever seen," I whispered severely.

Alexis had put on the white corset beneath her dress, it and her heels were all she wore; the panties had been left in my car. There was a coyness in how she held herself, but it was surface level.

I'd never known someone so genuine as her.

So *real*.

Perhaps that was why I'd become so obsessed with her. I couldn't have said during my many hours of frustrated mulling. I definitely couldn't have said now.

"It looks alright on me?" she asked, turning her body to try and examine herself. It was a pose that could have made anyone else look awkward. On her, it was a compelling flex of her body that made my fingers ache to not be touching her.

Sitting up fully, I motioned to her. "Get over here before I tackle you where you stand."

Light pink washed over her cheeks, the blush I loved so much. Making her react was addicting. I didn't think I could go on without that.

And I didn't plan to.

Alexis swayed my way, her hips tempting me with their gentle curves. Reaching out, I caught her by the wrist, pulling her on top of me. A tiny squeak escaped her surprised smile; sealing her lips, I ate her joy and longed for more.

This fucking woman... what was I going to do with this painful need for her?

What *could* I do?

Keep her by your side, I sang in my skull. *Never let her leave. Never let her dare to try.*

Alexis... my Pet...

She belonged to me.

"Silver," she whispered thickly. It wasn't my name. I'd had her use it from the start, because back then, I'd still had the delirious idea that I could satisfy my urge for this girl.

I'd had every intention of walking away when I was done... and I hadn't wanted her to know who I was, where I worked, any of it. It had always worked with the others.

Why not her?

"Take this off," she said. Bending against my bare chest, she scratched at the corset like it was choking her.

My smirk was a razor; she shivered at the sight. "Alright," I said, my hands caressing down her middle. I kissed her shoulder, then I inhaled her scent until my lungs threatened to burst.

One by one, I snapped the hooks on the front of the corset. The black vines decorating it wilted, peeling away to reveal the creamy expanse of her skin. Sucking at my own tongue, I yanked her so that she was sitting on my chest, rolling my cheek down her stomach.

She gasped, fingers tangling in my hair like she wanted to stop me, or force me to go faster. Could she be as swept up as I was? Was that even *possible?*

"Perfect," I said, circling the dip of her bellybutton. "Beautiful." My lips tattooed her bare hip, the corset parting like curtains on the most wonderful day. In front of me she was naked, but it wasn't *enough.*

I wanted to expose Alexis down to her soul.

Shoving her backwards so that her pussy hovered over my briefs, I shuddered. My shaft strained at the material, willing itself to break free so it could fill her up. Holding her hips, I ground her down, forcing her swollen clit to rub against my hard-on.

Throwing her head back, she moaned. The sound sank into me, fueling me, making my eyes darken. Lying below her, her breasts cast me in shadow. I'd have hidden from the sun for years if it was because of her.

To my surprise, she reached down, pulling my cock through the top of my briefs. I was almost too entranced to stop her, but before she could penetrate herself, I gripped her waist and held her still. Her frustrated wriggle was torture. "What are you doing?" I asked.

"Fucking you, or trying to."

I watched her with pure curiosity. "We need a condom."

The richness in her eyes warred with the green of her earrings. "Do we?"

Fucking hell.

She met my eyes—not with calmness, but with desire. "You'd risk carrying my child just to fuck me raw?"

Her fingers brushed mine, then went further, gripping the base of my cock. "Fuck me," she commanded.

"That's what I'm supposed to say." Pushing her hands away, I guided my stiff cock into her. She slid down on it slowly, groaning all the way until she was sitting on me. Gritting my jaw, I arched up, not satisfied with holding still.

Licking my thumb, I stroked her clit. She fell forward, hands on either side of my shoulders and her hair in my face. The sensation of the soft strands tickling over me was maddening.

Capturing the back of her head, I yanked her to my seeking teeth. We kissed violently, sharpness and force that was meant to satisfy a carnal, animal urge neither of us had experienced before.

I'd chased this feeling for so fucking long.

It had been here.

All along...

It had been with her.

Vindication gave me strength, my need to come drove me. The condo was filled with the wet sounds of our fucking. My Pet, she whimpered and moaned and even screamed. Not once was it an act.

"Silver, I'm so close. Fuck, I'm so close, please..."

Taking the hint, I circled her clit faster; harder. I played with her smoothly, never slowing down. I was as everlasting as any machine could have been.

Her pussy thrummed, sending hot ripples up my stomach. My balls flexed, sweat coating every inch of our bodies. Alexis was soaked, wetness escaping her perfect thighs and dripping down my cock.

Burying my face in the dip of her throat, I growled. Pressure exploded, my come filling her again and again. Still she squeezed me, like what I was giving her wouldn't be enough. She wanted me, *all* of me. Fuck, I was eager to give it up.

Together we slowed down, her weight settling on top of me. The symphony of her heart calmed me. The gentle sway of her lungs matched mine. We were synchronized in a way meant for old lovers.

For some time, neither of us spoke. I was too in my head, absorbing the reality of what was going on in my world. Was she thinking the same thing?

Alexis shifted, her eyes finding me through her drapery of hair. "Do you..." She stopped speaking.

"What?" I prompted her.

Looking to the side, her eyebrows crinkled ever slightly. "Nothing."

"No, tell me."

Alexis wasn't watching me, but she also wasn't looking at the wall. Where was she in her head? What did she see? "This thing we're doing," she whispered. "Have you done it before?"

Gently, I guided her off of me. We both winced when my cock slid free. "You're thinking about what Gerard said in the club." *That fucking asshole.* I'd come close to knocking him out just to shut him up.

Tucking her hair behind her ear, she shrugged. "I am. And I'm also not. I don't know." Her laugh cut into me. Right then, I thought I'd tell her anything—everything—if she only asked. "Am I just another girl you'll forget about?"

In front of me, she seemed to shrink. This wasn't the woman I knew. This was a stranger to me. The Alexis I wanted was strong... giving... and willing to put others before herself. Where had all that confidence gone?

My fingers brushed hers on the bed, making her look at me. "I could never forget you, Pet."

Her lips made the shape of an archer's bow. "Really?"

"Really," I said seriously.

Her green eyes sparkled, considering me dubiously. I must have passed her test, because the tension slid from her body in a great wave. She kissed me, a soft, quick thing that had as much impact as if it had lasted for hours.

I didn't speak anymore when she hugged me, and I didn't argue when she ran off to clean up in the bathroom. As I watched her slip out of view, her voice still chatting at me through the walls, I let my smile fade... and I endured the painful secret rolling in my skull.

I'd never forget Alexis. I knew I couldn't.
Because I'd already tried to.

- Chapter Eighteen -

Alexis

It was a bluish black throughout the condo. The giant curtains blocked all but the most bare fragments of the early light outside. It highlighted the smooth, strong shoulders and back that faced away from me.

Shifting gently so he wouldn't wake up, I stretched out on the pillow and just... watched him. I counted his breaths, how his ribs would flare and make his tattoos ripple like the sea. He was gorgeous when he was awake, but there was something beautiful about his sleeping face.

Peaceful, I realized. *I don't get to see him like that.*

It was too easy to stay there. Of course, my rumbling stomach became the first problem. My need to pee came second, and then my caffeine headache joined in.

Carefully, I slid out of the blankets. The bed didn't make a sound, it was one of those expensive brands that they brag about on TV, the kind where they'd show how good it was by jumping next to a glass of red wine on the mattress.

Ducking into the restroom, I navigated in the near-dark. When I was done, I tip-toed across the smooth wooden floors. Silver had bought me a pink "I Heart LA" hoodie from the airport; I snatched it from the suitcase, knowing the morning weather would be a little chilly, even here.

Tugging it over my messy hair, I winced as it caught the edge of my emerald earrings. I hadn't been able to take them off, they'd become a constant companion for me.

Hurrying to tie on my shoes, I gathered my phone and my purse and quietly snuck out the door. Riding the elevator, I smiled at myself in the mirror, humming a perky tune. I felt so *alive,* so fucking good!

Being with Silver was like taking a shot of adrenaline right to the heart.

I was nearly whistling by the time I was standing in line at the Starbucks right outside the condo. The barista slid me my change, then a grey tray with two paper cups of coffee stuck in it. *I hope Silver likes it black.* To be safe, I grabbed up a few packets of sugar. *Shit, is he a splenda guy, a raw sugar guy, what?*

My phone was buzzing. Sighing, I abandoned my sweetener crisis and used my free hand to dig out my cell. *Maybe it's Silver, wondering where I am.* My screen blew up with a myriad of texts. I didn't know the number... but reading the first sentence, I realized who they were from.

Unknown: Alexis, I'm sorry if I upset you. I don't know why you ran yesterday, but I'm sorry.

307

Unknown: And I'm sorry to send you this, because it might make it harder.

Unknown: But I need your help. I still believe you can be the key in this crime.

Unknown: This is the last thing I'll ask of you.

Detective Roose. I knew he had my number, but he'd never messaged me like this. The last text was a video. My thumb was pressing down before I even considered what he'd sent to me.

Instinct can be a real bastard.

On my screen, a black and white video rolled. I saw people standing around, the angle difficult to read any faces. It had to be security footage, a camera set in a high corner.

Then I saw myself.

Crushing the phone, I began to hyperventilate. I looked so young, a sweet and innocent eighteen year old. I was wearing a dress that I didn't recognize, a fluffy thing that made me glow in the video when compared to the rest of the muted world.

That's a dress I created!

The last one I'd ever made.

I was shaking so hard I nearly dropped my phone. My hand twinged; I was close to shutting it off, or throwing it so that it smashed forever.

No. No, this isn't...

It can't be.

I'd never once seen proof of that day five years ago. I'd tried to avoid the news, I never spoke to the police beyond my initial statement, and my therapist never pushed me too hard to discuss it... though I know she'd longed to.

But now, here it was. Real footage of the moment I'd worked so hard to bury deep in my psyche. Old me—old, confident, bold me.

As if I could sense myself in the future, the younger me glanced up, grazing over the camera. I saw my smile—and I saw the person approach me from behind as I waited in that bank line.

Then I remembered *everything*.

"Nice outfit," a voice said.

Laughing at the compliment, I spun towards the speaker. I was hoping someone would notice my clothing and say something. If I had any hope of getting accepted to a school for clothing design, I had to test the dresses in the wild and see if they stood out.

It was one of several I'd made to take with me when I left Portland.

"Thanks," I started to say. And then I stopped.

He smiled at me, his eyes glowing. Something was off, it took my brain a second to make sense of the puzzle in front of me. What was wrong with this man's face?

A mask. He was wearing a mask.

It was black, hiding everything but the pits of his richly amber eyes and his tense smile through the fabric. His finger came up, motioning for me to be quiet.

Then I saw the muzzle of the gun.

"Sorry," he whispered, training the weapon on me. "I wish there was another way."

I wanted to say, "Please." Or maybe, "Why me?" But I couldn't. I was frozen there as he whipped the gun high, warning everyone to stay back.

I was dead, I was going to die.

Fingers dug into my wrist, dragging me towards a wall. "Everyone get on the ground! And you," he said, pointing at a teller who had dared to lift a phone. "Tell the police I have hostages." He spoke with a harsh edge, muffled through the mask.

Huddling on the floor by his feet, I peered up as he started whispering to a different teller. In his fingers, a tiny black square shined. "Plug this into your computer," he snapped. "Hurry up."

"Okay, okay!" The teller fumbled with the thumb drive, but it must have gone in, because the robber nodded.

His gun clicked, a warning. "Stay there. No one will get hurt if no one moves." Crouching beside me, he slid out something the size of a cellphone, but it had too many buttons and wires.

The gun rested in his lap, still in his tight grip, and pointing near my feet.

I heard my own voice. "Don't do this, don't shoot anyone."

He eyed me, then went back to typing. "I won't if you all sit still."

"Is it money you want?"

His laugh was almost... tired. The vibrations of it shook my teeth to their roots. "I want everything."

"Here, just take this and leave us all alone." I dug into my purse, and in hindsight, I was lucky he didn't shoot me, because how could he know if I didn't have a weapon? "It's my bank info," I said, scribbling on a piece of paper. "My name, my PIN, everything. I've got almost fifty-thousand dollars, take what I have before the cops get here." I knew if the police arrived, there'd be shots fired for sure.

People would definitely die.

He was no longer tapping at his tiny device. Watching me like I was a new species, he eyed the paper, seeming to read it. Then, he stared at me again. "Why would you do this?"

"It's just money!" My voice came out louder than either of us was ready for; he flinched. "Why should anyone die because of it?"

"That's a question I've asked before." He took the paper from me, but just as my heart lifted, he tore it to shreds. "I don't want your money, Alexis Willow." Hearing my name sent ice shards into my gut. I'd written it down, of course he knew it. "I want someone else's."

"I don't understand," I said weakly.

"You don't have to." Then he flipped the device shut, nodding to himself. Rising, he motioned at the teller who hadn't budged. "Give me that back." Wordlessly, the man handed the black thumb drive over.

The stranger stood tall, his sunset-orange eyes raking the room, taking in every pale and twisted face. People who had families. People who weren't ready to die.

I saw him adjust the pistol, checking the clip. This was it, he was probably counting the

*bullets to see if there were enough for all of us.
I was going to be killed.*

And I needed to understand the reason.
"Why me?"

*The tip of his gun trained my way, the
black in his stare matching the gun's metal.
"Because I noticed you. That's the only
reason."*

That moment would change my life.

*With a final smile, he shoved me
towards the doors, his gun aiming into the air.
"Get out of here!" he roared at me—at
everyone. "You have two seconds before I start
firing on you!"*

*We all obeyed, stampeding out the front
in a torrent of acidic fear and panic.*

They'd never found him after that.
But he'd found me.

- Chapter Nineteen -

Alexis

It's funny, in hindsight, how many times I'd run from one man.

This time was *especially* funny, because now I was in the middle of LA with no money and no where to go. At least I was wearing shoes this time.

Ignoring how my chest was ripping open from my pushed-past-the-point-of-useful-lungs, I didn't stop moving until I was several blocks away from the condo.

Silver... how could he be the one that had held me hostage? How was it possible?

A mask had hid his face years ago, but my ears knew his voice. And his eyes... I'd spent enough time looking at them longingly. I'd mapped out who he *was*. I'd finally stopped thinking about him as some stranger I was infatuated with.

But I'd been wrong about him from the start.

He was never a stranger.

Something warm tickled my wrist. Shaking it off, I wiped at the coffee I'd spilled when I'd started sprinting. The paper cups and their little tray were both gone. *I must have dropped them.*

The only thing I still held onto was my phone. Dropping into a chair outside of a cafe, I took a huge breath—filled my lungs—then pressed play. And I kept pressing it. I sat there, ignoring every side-glance from the waiters and groggy customers, just rewatching the video until my eyes itched from not blinking.

All I'd had before was the sanitized version of the robbery from the News channels. As hard as I'd tried to avoid it all, it was impossible. I'd learned the robber had hacked the system from the inside. And my mother, who couldn't shut up about the event, had informed me that he'd not only stolen millions of dollars...

He'd given it all away.

Crodan Insurance Company had been the real victim in the attack. But their attempt to recover the money from their clients ended up revealing how they'd been screwing them all over for years.

Silver had given back what was owed to everyone from their corrupt policies. And I guess that had made it even harder to try and track down who had done the robbery, since the spoils had gone to every corner of the country.

People called it a Robin Hood act for a reason.

But what did I care about that? Silver had made me his fucking *pawn*. The glint of a gun and his smoldering voice had haunted the recesses of my nightmares for five years.

Silver had ruined my future.

But he didn't kill me.

Freezing, I paused the video. My own innocent smile looked back at me.

I'd never kissed a bullet. The only thing I'd ever kissed... was him.

Wiping my forehead, I shivered. Everything from my past and my present was getting contorted into a Gordian knot. Silver had threatened me, thrown me into a dark depression, ruined my confidence. He'd also come back into my life and exposed me to a new sense of self worth.

Which side of him was the real one?

And what the hell had made him come back to Portland to find me?

"Are you alright, Miss? Can I get you something?" One of the waiters had finally gotten brave enough to approach me. His tiny beard was slick and black, matching the one side of his hair that still remained.

Sitting up, I dropped my phone into my purse. The feeling of my wallet bumping my knuckles reminded me of my plight. *I have to get home.* I couldn't afford tickets out of here with my current funds.

It was awful, and also funny, when I considered it. Silver had been letting me lead this grand lifestyle with him. *With him.* On my own I was poor little Alexis Willow.

I smiled half-way at the waiter and said, "I'm fine. Really."

He didn't believe me, his stare tracking over my face. "Okay. Well, I can get you some water if you like."

"That'd be great." My run had dried me out.

Smiling politely, he looked me over once more, pausing. "Nice earrings, by the way."

Automatically, I reached for them. I must have looked silly with my mouth falling open. *The earrings.* "Hey!" I blurted. "You *can* help me, actually."

Cocking his head, he came a foot closer. "Tell me what I can do."

"Is there a pawn shop nearby?"

- Chapter Twenty -
Silver

Where the fuck was she.

Where the *fuck* was she.

WHERE THE FUCK WAS SHE!?

Stalking through my condo, I yanked on a pair of jeans with one hand. The other was busy hitting speed dial on her number for the tenth time. She wasn't picking up, but worse than that?

I had no clue where she could be.

Everything still smelled like her. Waking up to that scent while I twisted in her leftover warmth in the blankets had been exquisite.

Finding her side of the bed empty was torture.

"Pick up!" I growled at my cellphone, instantly tapping the call button again after it hit her voicemail. Had something happened to her? Why else was she not here?

There was a beep, then a mechanical voice telling me that, "The number you have reached..."

I slammed the phone onto my bed. I was lucky it didn't shatter, but fuck it, I could have bought a new one. I could buy anything.

Except for her.

She was gone.

Throwing the curtains open, I lit up the room. Alexis wasn't here, but still I looked. I had to be sure, I was praying I'd somehow missed her.

But I never miss anything.

Gripping my skull, I turned in place. *What the hell happened?* The night had ended perfectly—my cock buried up to its base in her sweet cunt, her mouth bruised from my kisses.

Relax. Maybe she went out to get coffee. I eyeballed the condo with a new purpose. *Yes, her sweater is gone. So are her shoes.* She'd walked out of here, that was clear. Was I over reacting?

No.

Pet's gone. I can't touch her.

I can't kiss her or feel her or SEE her.

I was reacting exactly like I should be.

Tugging on a shirt and my jacket, I stormed out the front door. Unless I was crazy, even the elevator smelled like her.

Pushing out into the open air, I scanned both ways while standing on the sidewalk. The Starbucks called to me, the air bitter with roasted beans. If she'd gone to get coffee, it would have been here.

Before I even got through the doors, something caught my eye. There was a greyish item on the ground, a puddle shining as it absorbed into the street. With my heart racing, I knelt by the mess. One paper cup was still in the tray, the other was open on its side.

I wasn't a bloodhound, but unquestionably, this was a sign.

My legs cut over the ground and into the shop. The woman behind the counter saw me coming, her eyes widening like I was death on a damn pale horse.

Maybe I was.

It depended on what she was about to tell me.

"I'm looking for someone," I said, cutting to the chase. "About your height, sharp green eyes, long dark hair. Probably wearing a pink sweatshirt."

She balked, chewing her bottom lip. "Oh, uh. Was it one of those "I heart" or "I love" or something LA shirts?"

Choking on bile, I crushed my nails into my palms. "What happened to her?"

She darted a look around, as if I was about to announce I was pranking her and this was a TV show. But my intensity was nothing to laugh at. "I don't really know, honestly. She was here maybe fifteen minutes ago, maybe half an hour? She ordered some drinks, then she just ran off. She looked really scared, man."

Scared.

My head was swimming, tipping like I could reveal the answer if I just swung my brain around hard enough. "What way did she go?"

"Up ninth," she said. I was already moving, so her next words were louder. "Should I call the cops? Was she like, your girlfriend or something?"

Yes. I thought, but I didn't speak.

I needed all my energy to run.

- Chapter Twenty-one -

Alexis

Rubbing the inside of my ear, I worked my jaw. I wasn't much of a flier, yet I'd been on two different planes in just two days. While it was exciting to be in the sky, I could live without the crunching crackle of my ears popping.

I could have also gone for the roomier seats of a certain fancy jet. Being squished against the window wasn't as glamorous as the recliners had been. *But so what?* I asked myself grimly. *I'd ride a rabid donkey before I'd sit next to him ever again.*

Hours after learning that Silver was the man from my past, I was still just as angry. My phone battery had died from how many times I'd replayed the video during the flight. That was for the best, since I wasn't doing a good job controlling the compulsive need to torture myself.

However, the downside was that—since I'd been forced to fly with multiple layovers—I had nothing to take my mind off of things. Each flight, I'd sit and browse the same magazine the airline stuck in the back-seat fold. In each airport, I'd wander around aimlessly, wishing I had a charger for my phone.

When we finally touched down in Portland, it was dark outside.

Climbing into a taxi, I slumped in the backseat and, except when the driver asked where I lived, didn't speak the whole ride. It should have felt good to be home. It only made me feel worse.

I was weary, my joints ached. This was supposed to be my second day kicking around LA. Instead I was here, dragging myself up my cracked walkway, past the rotting stench of the dumpster. When I came close enough to set my automatic porch light off, I saw something crumpled on the ground.

It was a half-eaten dead mouse.

Swallowing down a wave of nausea, I peeled my purse open. Lifting the keys high, I struggled with the door. I started to shove on it, baffled when the knob didn't move. My door was as solid as a wall.

What the fuck? Blinking, I turned the keys in my hand. I didn't recognize them at all —and then I did. Silver had handed me copies of his, I'd completely forgotten.

Shaking my head to clear the webbing, I finally found my keys and let myself inside. Carelessly, I dropped my purse on the floor. The pink sweater soon followed, landing somewhere—I wasn't really watching.

Plugging my phone into my charger beside the kitchen table, I filled a tea kettle with water. I was setting it on the stove, the blue flames clicking on, when I heard the first 'beep.' On autopilot, I lifted my phone.

Twenty-two missed calls.

All from Silver.

Running my thumb over the edge of the device, I hesitated. *Don't talk to him. Don't even read his messages.*

What could he say that could change how much I hated him?

Nothing.

Not a word.

Yet still, I opened the texts.

Silver: Talk to me, please.

Silver: Where are you?

Silver: Tell me you're okay.

Silver: Pet, answer me.

Silver: Did something happen?

Silver: Did I happen?

Silver: If someone hurt you, I'll kill them.

Tensing up, I read that last text again. *The one who hurt me was you,* I thought. Reading his words sent shame tumbling into my wall of betrayal. *I should have told him I flew home. What if he thinks I'm in LA and something happened to me?*

He must be so worried, so lost and confused. It wasn't my problem, but...

Pushing the phone to my forehead, I groaned. "No," I said to myself. I needed to hear my own voice out loud. "He fucked up—he beyond fucked up. That guy could have killed me! He nearly did! I don't want to talk to him at all. Never."

Never was a sharp word, it made me tense up.

Against my skull, my phone vibrated. Startled, I pulled away, watching as a new message appeared in stark black letters.

Silver: I won't leave you alone until you tell me you're alright. Not knowing is worse than death, Pet. Talk to me.

Crumbling into a chair, I saw myself from a distance. One by one, I typed the letters on my phone. I was justifying my reasons, saying to myself, *He deserves to know that I hate him.* Wouldn't that feel good?

My text said: Don't ever contact me again.

The kettle started to whistle, fraying my already raw nerves. Jumping up, I rattled the cups over the sink. The tea was too hot to drink, so I leaned over it and breathed in the steam.

It'll be okay.

Everything will be okay.

My phone started blowing up, message after message hammering at me. They came so fast that I backed away, gawking at the device as it vibrated madly. Silver was desperate to reach me.

I snatched up my cell and turned it off. The sudden silence was heavy, unnatural. Listening to my breathing, I grabbed the table and worked at calming down.

In all things, Silver was demanding. He didn't care that I'd instructed him to leave me alone. I had a chilling feeling that this wouldn't be the end of it.

Of us.

Ignore him, change your number, whatever it takes. I was never going to see that man again.

Walking through the living room, I paused. The pink LA sweater was sitting on a chair where I'd dropped it. *Throw it away.* Stepping closer, I squinted at the shiny laminated letters. *You threw away his gifts before. This will be easy.*

Do it!

Clutching my tea, I walked closer to the sweater... and I kept going.

I'd done many things to block Silver from my life. I'd even sold the earrings that I'd loved—the very first gift he'd sent me—just to get away from him.

I told myself that I didn't need to do more.

So I only had myself to blame when I woke up smelling him.

The source was easy to find; I still had the jacket he'd draped over me the night I'd run from his apartment. Fingering the collar, I slid my palm down the sleeve. What was I going to do, give it back to him?

Fondling the buttons, I stopped. It was too easy to remember him wearing this, how it stretched over his broad body, or how he'd play with the cuffs and make me think of him playing with me.

Deep in the pocket, I found the business card. I'd left it there after discovering it, not sure what to do with the thing. Bending a corner, I read the printed words. *Keswick Silverwell.* I knew where he worked, maybe I could send the jacket back to him. That would let me avoid him entirely.

Stalled by indecision, I took the easy road—I would do nothing today.

I'd have time to decide.

Finishing my morning routine, I marveled at how he consumed me even now. My home was full of him, my head just as stuffed. Silver—Keswick—whatever I called him, he was firmly under my flesh.

I'll forget him. Eventually... I'll forget him.

Driving my car to work wasn't the escape I hoped for. I struggled to think about my day, or about navigating the low-mist of rain. When I parked my car twenty minutes later, he was still an echo in my head.

By the end of today, it'll be easier. It had to get easier. All I needed was time... space... distance. Lifting my eyes, I scanned the front steps of my workplace.

Silver was waiting for me.

I pulled up short, freezing where I was, trapped under the intensity of his stare. He was wearing a shiny leather jacket, the material slick from the light drizzle.

He took a step, then another, and I was still frozen. It wasn't until he reached for me that the spell broke.

"Pet," he said, blinking as I backed away.

"I told you to leave me alone."

"You did," he agreed, his voice low and haunting. "But I can't. Not until I know why... and maybe not even then."

I thrilled at how he phrased that, then I snuffed out the damn fire in me with a cold reminder. "You *know* why! There's no way you don't know what you did!"

All at once, his face fell. I was looking at a lifeless statue. "You remember," he whispered.

"Yes," I said. "I fucking remember."

His arms were long enough to grab my shoulders. "Let me explain, Pet—"

"Don't call me that!" Wrenching away, I struggled to keep tears from my eyes. Around us, people slowed, listening but pretending not to. To them we were a couple having a spat, but I knew we were so much more.

Something akin to pain flooded his vision. His fingers hovered in the air, willing me to come back. "I won't walk away from you. I'm not going to vanish, not after everything. Let me talk to you."

"You're wasting your time. I don't want to hear another word."

"If you'd—"

"*I said leave me alone!*"

His eyebrows ran low, then he glanced over my shoulder. I started to turn, hearing Detective Roose before I saw him. "Miss Willow," he said, walking up to stand beside me. His voice was light, not matching how fiercely he stared at Silver. "What's going on here?"

Sweat spread over the back of my neck. Glancing between the men, I understood the root of my fear. Here, right in front of Roose, was the man he'd been searching for. I'd done what he'd hoped; I'd led him right fucking to him.

It would have taken no effort to say, "That's the guy who hacked Old Stone." The surface of my tongue was too parched to make

338

a sound. I wasn't scared for me, though... I was scared for Silver.

I don't want him to go to jail.

He was the robber! He'd held me hostage! He'd ruined *everything* for me. Why were my guts rolling with unease at being the one to expose him to the public?

Because you still care about him. Even if you don't want to.

This would be my last act of kindness. I'd use it to make sure Silver left me alone forever. "Nothing is wrong, *Detective.*" I emphasized that last word.

Silver snapped his eyes to me, then back to Roose.

I said, "This guy thought I was someone he knew. But we cleared it up."

"That so?" The detective rocked on his heels, flipping his coat back so that we could all see the shape of the gun holster at his hip. He was reading our interaction so easily, he could tell there was animosity brewing here.

Silver hadn't twitched. Not even his eyelashes moved. The heavy silence was broken only by the occasional rumble in the sky. The clouds were warning that the drizzle was going to get much worse.

I hoped that my warning to Silver was just as obvious.

Leave me alone, get out of here before Roose senses who you are. On some level I knew that was impossible, but my nerves said otherwise. I still didn't know why the hell I cared what happened to Silver, I just... did.

The sooner he left, the sooner I could stop thinking about him.

Lifting his chin, he focused his amber eyes on me. "Yes," he said softly. "Everything is clear now."

Barbed wire circled my heart, shredding it.

With a slow smirk aimed at Roose, he showed us both the back of his jacket. Quickly, he flicked up his collar. It only hid his neck, but that action felt like he was cutting himself off from me.

Stop letting him get to you. It was a firm, logical plea. This was what I'd wanted, I needed Silver to get out of my life. He was a bastard, a mad man, a fucking dream-killer.

But as I watched him fade slowly into the wet, foggy distance, the thorns in my chest dug deeper. I might have pushed off my heels and chased after him, except Detective Roose moved first.

"Did you get my messages?" he asked.

"Yeah," I said, watching as the man I'd wrapped myself up in became a black speck.

"And did they shake anything loose for you? Did you remember anything?"

Silver turned the corner, gone.

"Alexis?"

Looking up at Roose, I slid damp hair from my face. "No, sorry. I didn't remember anything."

The wrinkles in his face grew, making him look so much older. "Damn. That was my last shot." He squinted closer at me. "Don't feel too badly, okay?"

I must have been looking grim. Shaking myself, I fought to put on a new smile. "I wish I could have helped you more."

"You did help me." Confused, I gave him my full attention. "The answer isn't always as obvious as we'd like. So you don't recall the robbery, fine. That just means I have to work harder. And maybe that's what was always needed to crack this case. Nothing wrong with a little hard work, right?"

"Right," I whispered.

"It wasn't a waste of time," he said firmly. He stood over me, the thick clouds behind his head starting to lighten up. "I'm glad I got to meet you, Alexis. You made me think about everything a little differently."

"I did?"

"Yeah." Flashing his teeth, he winked. "And honestly, I think being forced to dig into your past must have helped you, too. When I met you a few weeks ago, you were... I don't want to sound like a dick, but you were kind of fragile. I don't get that same vibe anymore."

Rain tickled my eyelashes, I didn't wipe it away. *What is he talking about?*

"Anyway," he said, looking over his shoulder at the sky. "Thanks for trying. It means a lot. And... would you look at that beautiful sight?" He walked away from me for a few steps. "Rain is stopping, sun is shining, and I have an assload of paperwork to get on. See ya, Alexis."

Lifting my arm, I spoke with determination. "Bye, Vermont."

He stopped short, his mouth opening in surprise. I knew calling him by his first name would make him happy. He deserved that.

With a final wave, he strolled down the sidewalk.

The sky was cutting through the clouds, ignoring the blacker bits that still lingered in the distance. Long after the detective was out of sight, I stood on those wet steps and thought about what he'd said.

No longer fragile...

When I finally went inside, the puddles were gone.

- Chapter Twenty-two -
Alexis

"Mom, please," I groaned. "I don't want to talk about this."

"But honey," her voice chopped through my phone. "Just tell me what went wrong. It had to be pretty bad to break up with a guy who could fly you all the way to LA for a weekend!"

Hunching over my steering wheel, I again regretted picking up the phone. "Why don't you want to believe me when I say he messed up?"

She clicked her tongue. "Lexi, I'm just saying that... well... maybe you should reconsider."

"Reconsider?" I spit the word out.

"You're no spring chicken, dear. Why not settle down with a nice rich man like him and..."

Turning a little harder than I needed to, I debated dropping my phone on the floor of the car. "Mom. Look. You're fixated on all the wrong things."

"Money isn't ever wrong."

"I never cared about the money!" The rubber under my hands squeaked from the pressure of my grip. I was about to say more, when the low murmur of my radio slid into my awareness.

The voice in my speakers said, "...Just like years ago, and prompting the bank..."

I turned the radio dial upwards.

"But Alexis, just give him a chance, you aren't getting any young—"

"I need to go." Clicking the end call button, I dropped my phone into the cupholder and cranked the radio even louder. The person talking—some news station announcer —filled the air. "Authorities are saying there's still no suspect. Here's officer Santile with more details."

Santile? That was the cop who'd driven me home the night Silver and I had... *Don't think about that. Or him.*

"We're still looking over video and talking to witnesses," Santile said, sounding more severe than he had when he'd helped me. "But the issue comes with the way the robbery happened. We know it occurred sometime around two in the morning. We know no one entered the Goldman Bank, or left it. It seems to have happened entirely through the computer system itself."

Gripping the wheel, I steered my car into the breakdown lane. Passing drivers honked at me, but I ignored them. *Silver. He did it again.*

The voices on the radio went sketchy, breaking up. I twisted the knob, but it didn't help, the radio waves were junk. I was

347

regretting my shit-can car when the first speaker came back. "That was Officer Santile. If you have any information about the crime, please call their hotline. The number is one-eight-eight…"

I dropped my forehead against my knuckles. *Why did he do it? It's like my mom said, isn't he already rich?* Was this a game to him, what would make him risk getting caught?

They said no one entered or left. Last time, he used a little device he had the teller plug in at the bank. He must have gotten better over the years, he didn't even *need* to show up in person to perform the hack this time.

Sitting tall, I arched my neck and looked at my ceiling. *This has nothing to do with me.* Even thinking that, guilt still knotted in my stomach. It had become my familiar friend these days.

Pulling out into traffic, I finished the drive to the post office in deep thought.

When I entered the tiny building, Kerie waved at me from behind the counter. I returned the gesture, my mail-key jingling in my lock. Cracking the door, I reached in to grab the few envelopes... and stopped.

There was a letter waiting for me.

First came shock, then came fury. *I told him to leave me alone!* Grabbing the paper, I read the perfectly curling ink. It said only one thing, *Pet*.

Trembling, I ripped it open.

Pet,

You told me to leave you alone. I think you know that I can't.

I'm going to do everything I can to get you back in my grip, I need to touch you so badly, I—

Crushing the letter, I threw it on the ground and fucking *screamed*.

Why was he still reaching out to me? He was insane—he had to be. Wasn't it clear after seeing me with Detective Roose that talking to me was stupid? It was the riskiest thing he could do, especially after I'd warned him off, and *still* he was doing it!

"Hey!" Kerie said, breaking into my thoughts. "Are you okay?"

Freezing, I looked around without moving my head. Everyone was watching me, their unease plain as day. For once, I didn't care. Let them stare, I was tired of holding my emotions inside.

He's putting himself in danger just to talk to me.

Through the frustration, there was a twang of remorse... and longing.

Kerie waved his hands gently, his voice hushed. "Calm down, you're freaking everyone out. What happened?"

"Nothing," I said, rolling my shoulders. I bent down to scoop up the letter, but Kerie beat me to it. "Wait!"

Ignoring me, he unfolded the mess, eyes scanning the page. "Oh, jeez," he sputtered. Flicking me a quick look, he read more. "Uh, wow. This is from that guy, huh?"

Burning down to my feet, I snatched it back from him. "Pretend you didn't read that."

Understanding glimmered in his eyes. "You're pissed at him, aren't you?"

"Was it obvious?" Sighing, I fluffed my hair. "Sorry, that came out mean. I'm just... I didn't expect him to write to me again."

"Oh. That's probably why he paid me extra to give you this."

Stunned, I looked down at the small black satchel Kerie held. I couldn't make myself reach out and touch it. "Why did he give you that?"

Pointedly, he nodded at the crushed letter. "I'm guessing he figured you'd react like that and didn't want whatever this is to get ruined."

Silver was too smart for his own damn good.

But not smart enough to leave me alone.

Shaking, I opened and closed my hands at my sides. My instinct said to take the gift and see what it was. The alarmingly sharp part of my mind said to walk away and stand firm. Silver was trying to buy me back.

I wouldn't let him.

"Hey!" he shouted, chasing after me as I stormed out to my car. "Where are you going?"

"He's determined to get me to talk to him." Climbing into the driver's seat, I revved the engine. "I'll give him what he wants."

Kerie inched forward, then back again. I wouldn't have run him over, but he was acting like I might. "What the hell happened between you two?"

I spared him a single glance. "Everything."

And it was the truth.

When he moved out of my way, I burned rubber in my wake.

- Chapter Twenty-three -
Alexis

A business card and Silver's jacket were my only companions in the car. I'd stopped at my place just long enough to grab them.

Touching the jacket had been a shocker. His essence was all over it, and the weight reminded me too much of how his hands felt on my shoulders.

Parking my car, I went to pick up the jacket... and I stopped.

Am I really doing this?

In the mirror, I saw the circles under my eyes. Kicking Silver out of my life had been a futile effort. I couldn't sleep because he was a constant in my dreams. Waking with the memory of his touch was torture.

Running away had always been the answer to my problems. Except it had never solved anything. It had taken me years to realize that.

The only way to end this is to face him.

With great control, I scooped his jacket up and climbed out into the purple light of the evening. Lifting my eyes, I stared at the building. It was blackened stone, modern-style windows running down the front like buttons on a suit. It had a buzz that just screamed *money.*

Money and sex.

Pushing my hand against the door, I walked into Pure Pleasure Incorporated.

The waiting room was glossy white, a series of small, round chairs set to one side. There was a water cooler as well as an impressive little machine that seemed to make single cups of coffee or tea. One man was mixing a drink as I watched.

I knew instantly that this wasn't a place people just walked into. Pure Pleasure didn't sell their products here, they *made* them here.

I probably look like a tourist. But tourists didn't have the singular intensity in their eyes like I did.

The statuesque and painfully gorgeous red-head behind the front desk waved at me. "Can I help you?" she asked.

Stepping forward, my eyes tracked along the nearby hallway. Was he down there? "I'm looking for..." I nearly spilled the name *Silver*. "Keswick. Is he here?"

"Mr. Silverwell?" she asked, her pouty lips scrunching tight. She flicked her eyes down to the jacket I was holding. Did she recognize it? Then, she gave his location away by peeking over her shoulder. "Um, let me just make a call and see if—"

I was already marching down the hallway.

"Hey!" she shouted, following behind me. "Wait! You can't just go down there!"

Watch me. Clenching my hands, I moved faster. I was done not understanding his motives.

I was going to get answers.

And I was getting them *now*.

Rounding the corner, I entered a new room. It was big and wide, a long staircase crawling up the other side. Computers filled several counters, people hunched and typing away. Some were drawing on gigantic screens, and one look had me blushing.

Dildos are obvious from any distance.

Everything was a whirl of faces and colors, a low murmur of music and voices. This was no sweatshop, people were smiling and joking from their chairs as they worked.

"Excuse me, Miss!"

Ignoring her, I spun on my heel, head swinging. *Where is he?* He had to be here, I was sure. So why didn't I see him?

"You need to...!" She reached for me; I darted away, infuriating her further and not caring one bit. I didn't feel like myself, I'd slid out of my own skin somewhere along the way. The old me, the shivering and traumatized me, was on the sidewalk outside.

His face was turned away, speaking to someone who was hunched over their laptop.

But I knew him with miles between us.

Silver lifted his eyes, catching me from the corner of one. I watched with amazement as his sure smile shattered. I saw it drip lower and lower, almost sliding from his jawline.

The person sitting next to him perked up, sensing Silver's sudden change in mood. The other man twisted his chair, looking between us curiously.

Pet, Silver mouthed, but no sound came out. It should have felt so fucking *good* to see him shocked. But standing there under his powerful stare, I began drifting.

Hold on, I told myself. My internal voice was hollow. *Focus, get angry! He ruined everything you were! You need to hate him!*

In my chest, something clutched my heart and squeezed.

Neither of us had moved. His toes pointed at me, his hands—hands that had always been unexpectedly soft—clenching at his hips. He was coiled all the way to his eyebrows, and even so, frozen to the ground.

I could feel every breath he took, my own body swelling simultaneously.

"What are you doing here?" he asked, danger flashing through his tone.

"I'm sorry, sir." My red-headed pursuer came around, her phone lifted calculatingly. "I tried to stop her, but she just ran back here! I'll call the police."

"Wait," he said, motioning for her to stop. "It's fine."

I felt a twinge of delight at how her mouth flapped. "Sir?"

Silver hadn't stopped watching me. I was rooted to the spot, digging for any fragment of the strength I'd stormed in with. *Remember who he is.* Cutting into my own palms with my nails, I steeled myself. "We need to talk."

He eyed me closely. I could feel his pupils trying to slip into my head and understand why I was here. "My office," he said, gesturing at the stairs. Then he turned enough to talk to the man at the computer. "Florian, send that data to me and I'll finish looking it over."

"Alright," the blonde stranger said. He squinted at me again, like he could grasp what was going on if he looked hard enough.

The woman from the front desk stood there another minute. I think she kept expecting Silver to change his mind and tell her to call security after all.

Of course, he didn't.

The office was gorgeous, high ceilings, tall windows, and a black couch that glistened in the corner. Silver shut the door behind us; the lock clanked through the air pointedly. "How did you find me?" he snapped.

"I thought you'd be happy," I said, not hiding my sarcasm. "You wanted to see me, here I am."

"You know I didn't mean like this." Running a palm over his hair, he stayed by the door. The tension in his face made me realize that as big as this office was, there was little space between us.

"Your business card," I said, shaking his jacket. "It was in the pocket, *Keswick*." I spit his real name out, then threw the garment onto the floor by his desk.

Silver's shoulders slid down. "Of course." He relaxed enough to prop himself on the wall, one knee bent—oddly casual. "I'm guessing you didn't come here just to return that."

"Of course not!" Filling my chest, I threw my arms down. "I told you to leave me alone, but you still keep trying to reach me! More letters, more fucking *gifts?* I never wanted to see your face ever again, Silver!" *Lies.* "But I'm here, so talk. Tell me why you're risking your safety by contacting me—*me,* who you know has been talking to the detective who wants to put you in prison!"

His mouth became a thin line. It was his only reaction.

I said, "I need to understand. I can't handle knowing you're out here, waiting for me... thinking of me... until I know why you came back in the first place."

His next movements were too fast, his body rushing forward until he had me backed against the polished desk. "You don't understand yet, do you, Pet?"

"Don't call me Pet." It was a frail demand, so I narrowed my eyes. Fuck, he was too close. His heat was washing over me, and with the sharp edge of the desk behind me, I was trapped. "*Hostage* is better, isn't it?"

I meant to piss him off. Amazingly, a slow smirk spread over his lips. "I'll call you that if you want. My hostage, I fucking love that. It means you're *mine*."

Hot ripples made my lower belly squeeze. *No, don't let him get to you.* This man was a demon crafted from sexual desire. I had to be strong, I needed to understand what was going on. "I remember everything, you know. That means I remember how you nearly killed me."

His eyebrows scrunched.

I didn't let him speak, my lips curling back as my anger returned. "You put a gun to my fucking head. I thought I was going to *die,* Silver! I was ready to go out into the world and live my life and you stole that *away from me!*"

My muscles bunched, I shoved forward and pushed him off of me. The baffled light that entered his eyes was glorious. I'd never felt so powerful, so... so *right.*

"I was never going to pull the trigger—"

"How could I know that? Why does that even matter?"

"You weren't in real danger, Pet, I—"

"I said don't call me that!" I jabbed a finger at him. "Because of you, my whole life went off the rails!" Infused by fury, I pushed him back further.

Hard fingers coiled in my hair. My world spun, his force spinning me so that I bounced against the door. I felt the hinges rattle along with my teeth. It didn't hurt, but it left me stunned.

Silver's nose ground on mine, his searing words kissing my ears. "You're accusing me of planning to kill you when you won't even *listen* to my side." He tightened his hands, breathing faster—deeper. "You said you wanted to know why I came to this city, why I came back for you."

Hot tears of exhaustion prickled the corners of my eyes. "Was it to destroy what was left of me? Is that why you've been playing with me, so you could twist me up inside and fuck me over? You broke me, you fucking *broke me! Why did you come back?!*"

His teeth bruised me as his kiss smothered my mind. Pleasure and pain sponged through my skin. I was ready for war, not for this. I wanted to hate him, and in a way, I still did. But betrayal wasn't enough to lock my senses away from someone like him.

I gasped for air when he freed me. The fervor in his eyes was disorienting, I had the strangest suspicion that he was just as lost as I was. "You," he hissed out, the word as permanent as a tattoo on his flesh. "I came back because of *you.*"

My blink was sluggish; I struggled in his grip, yet he just squeezed me harder. "That isn't an answer, I want a real answer!"

His whole face crumbled, I saw his molars as he shouted. "I couldn't stop thinking about you! Is that what you need to hear?"

Quicker and quicker, I was floating away from my own body.

What does he mean?

He spat out more words, each coming hotter—more furious—than the last. "I couldn't get you out of my mind!" Laughing, Silver cupped his temples and backed away. "And then you went and forgot about *me*."

I slumped on the wall, my knees giving out until I sank to the floor. "I don't... I don't understand."

"Neither do I." Rubbing the bridge of his nose, Silver backed up into his desk so violently it shook. His nameplate fell to the floor, ignored entirely. "Why would a girl I'd met for a few mere minutes be hammered into my skull?"

He wasn't watching me. It was one of the few moments where he wasn't. Able to study the curve of his nose and the way his hair faded down his temples, I thought he looked exceptionally tired.

Then he jabbed his eyes back at me, and I jumped. "Do you want to know what I figured out?" he asked.

"Please," I said on impulse.

He smiled with one side of his mouth. "I like that word on your lips." His chest flared, like he was gathering himself. "This is what I know. That day we met—that fateful little moment? I was at the climax of finally getting the revenge I'd been desperate for. I had no intention of staying in this city once I was done. I was ready to forget everything."

Every answer he spit just gave me new questions. I didn't want to stop the flow of information I was getting, so I sat on my hands and listened quietly.

Silver said, "A year after robbing those bastards, you still lingered in my thoughts. Fuck, it was frustrating!" Laughing without humor, he hung his head. He was speaking to the floor, or maybe himself. I felt like an observer. "You were no one, and I was becoming *someone*. I used money and my growing power to invest in more of both. It was easy, and finding women to distract myself with was even easier."

A splinter of disgust stabbed into me. *Stop. Fucking stop.* I was here for answers, not to question if learning the truth would divide Silver and me even more. I didn't *want* to be connected! He'd wronged me... and I had to keep that in my heart.

I had to.

"No matter how many girls I screwed, though... at the end of everything, as I fell asleep or my mind wandered, you were there." He lifted his eyes, burning me like an ageless sun. "*You*, Alexis Willow. The girl from my past."

My blood flash-flooded my veins, making my heart pound.

In the recess of his voice, I sensed his sincerity. "I knew I had to make you my present."

Clutching at the sides of my knees, I summoned pain, fear, anything to smother my rising delight. No matter how I tried, I couldn't get my rage to clog the path to my soul.

My voice cracked. "You came back just to be with me?" A wave of light-headedness made me sway where I sat. "How did you even find me?"

"I had your name." He cracked a wider grin. "I've got some talent with using information, remember? I'm the infamous hacker that got away." It should have felt like he was bragging. It didn't. "I've been watching you for so long, trying to grasp what made you so chronically addicting."

"So you *were* stalking me," I whispered.

"Yes. When you asked me that on our first date, I was surprised."

First date? "I still don't understand. What did I *do* to you?" How had I affected this bold, impossibly forceful man?

370

Silver leaned forward. His fingers crushed the rim of the desk, knuckles turning white. "That day in the bank, do you remember what we talked about?"

"I don't know. I really don't."

"Money, right?"

I breathed out through my nose. "Yes. You were robbing the damn bank, of course it was about money."

He chuckled, and the sound made me stare at him. "Not *my* money. Yours. Alexis, you offered me everything you had."

Had I done that? Digging back, I remembered what he meant. I'd handed him my bank info, imploring him to take the money I'd set aside. I'd wanted him to leave everyone alone, flee before an errant bullet was fired from him or a brave cop.

Silver gripped the desk harder, I waited for the wood to splinter. "You needed that money, didn't you?"

"It was going to be for college. For leaving the city." Acid bubbled on my tongue. "I spent it all on therapy instead. It took me forever to handle my anxiety well enough to get a fucking job."

"Because of me." It wasn't a question.

"Because of you, yes."

His eyes were hooded, no light touching the black centers. The sun hit him from behind, extending his shadow so that as it stretched over the room, floating an inch from me on the rug.

Finally, he must have realized what he'd done to me years ago. What he was *still* doing by continuing to reach out to me. Did he feel regret? Did he feel anything at all?

Silver's voice was so low that I had to strain to hear him. "You were the first person I'd ever met that knew that money wasn't as important as someone's life." His chin touched his chest, I couldn't see his expression. "I'll say it again. I never planned to hurt you that day."

With great effort, I kept myself steady. "What about now?"

His eyes shot up, raw and wild. "Excuse me?"

Silver had hacked another bank, the radio had told me. If the first hadn't been enough, why was this one any different? There was a chance people would get caught in the middle the longer he was on the streets.

People who might not be lucky enough to survive with *just* emotional scars, like me.

My stomach ate itself as I weighed my question. "Do you even think about anyone else, or do you just want more money?"

"Why would I..." He locked up. "Ah. You've been watching the news."

Pulling my numb hands up, I gestured around the luxurious office. "You have all this, why are you stealing more?"

"You're right, I'm rich. Why *would* I rob anyone?"

He was challenging me to come up with a reason. As I hunched there, my hands balling into fists... I slowly let my arms drift to the floor. He was right, why would he risk robbing another bank if he didn't need the money?

Licking my lips, I said, "You wouldn't. You're saying it's not you."

A flicker of relief glowed in his handsome face. He was happy I believed him. "It's not me. Though I'd love to know who it is."

Rattled by all this information, I cradled my head in my hands. Silver had led me on the road to hell, he'd stolen my confidence and I'd wallowed in the despair of that for years. But who I'd been back then... and who I was now... was as different as night and day. I'd changed again and again.

What about him?

Before I could react, his long arms curled around my huddled body. Everything in him flexed, he lifted me like I weighed nothing. The front of his shirt brushed my cheek, his scent comforting me.

Sitting back on the desk, he held me tight in his lap. "Do you believe me, that I wouldn't hurt you?" His lips were so close. So damn close.

He saw me staring, following the energy that connected between our bodies. "I'm not sure."

Silver cracked a surprising smile. "That honesty again. Then how about this." The same fingers that had dug into his desk gently rolled down my cheek. "I'm going to prove to you that you're safe with me."

A layer of tingles moved with his hand. "How?"

"By spending every waking moment— and some non-waking ones—at your side." The sunlight flared behind him, finally catching the edges of his perfect teeth. "I told you before. Now that I have you back, I'm never letting you go." He nuzzled my ear, eliciting a whimper. "My beautiful hostage. My *Pet.*"

"I have so many more questions," I said, turning his way.

"You know so much already, what else is there?"

I watched him from under my eyelashes. "You said I forgot you. But the you that I knew back then... he was a monster. Did you really want me to remember that?"

"No, not at all. Selfish or not, I never wanted you to remember that day. In just a few months, we've created something so hot, so addicting between us." He nuzzled the hollow of my throat. "For awhile, I'd hoped I could satisfy my curiosity with you... and then forget you."

I hugged him harder.

"But I couldn't do it. I couldn't shake you off. When you remembered who I was, I was distraught, and also happy. You finally knew me. I didn't have to hide anymore. What finally jogged your memory?"

The reminder of the video on my phone had me tensing up all over again. Silver sensed it, embracing me like he could squeeze the pain away. "That guy who was facing off with you outside my work, Detective Roose? He sent me a video of the robbery."

"Is that so," he mused softly.

Eyeing him, I was reminded of one of the reasons I'd come here. "He's been talking to me for weeks. He really wants to find you, Silver." Ice settled in my veins. "You have to be more careful."

"I'm very careful."

"No you aren't! You kept talking to me even when I told you not to!" Under my barrage of words, his expression was calm. The corner of his mouth was begging me to kiss it, his eyes warm as an Indian summer. "Weren't you worried I'd turn you in to the police?"

Running a knuckle across my forehead, he brushed my earlobe. "When you're in love, you stop caring about the risks."

Love.

My heart took all of my focus. It spun and swelled, it possessed my mind.

Love.

Heat settled in my skin, my vision focusing solely on Silver. "You love me?" I whispered.

"If you hadn't figured that out by now," he said, cupping the back of my head. "Then I've done a very poor job." Stroking my hair, he cradled me against him. "I'll never forgive myself for being the one that fucked up your life."

Shoving him back on the desk, I kissed him while he was still stiff with shock. He'd expected a longer battle with me, for us to create new scars.

I spoke against the softness of his lips. "You *did* fuck everything up. You tore my world apart and left me in pieces. But ever since you came back into my life... I've become someone braver, bolder, and more confident than I'd ever dared to be before." My fingers linked with his. "How could I not love you for that?"

There was no hesitation in how he pulled me to him. We'd already been touching, but somehow, he compressed us until our hearts were fighting to become one. I wanted to laugh, to fucking cry, to dance on the desk and then scream the news down at his employees.

I was in love with the man who'd destroyed me.

How fitting that he'd be the one to put me back together again.

- Chapter Twenty-four -
Silver

She entered the room like a princess from another time. It wasn't her dress—that was purple and hugged her tight—and it wasn't a crown—she hadn't even done her hair up. No, Alexis just glowed with the serenity of someone who could draw every eye and never even realize it.

As sweet as she looked, there was no hiding the womanly way she walked. My cock twitched when she brushed her hands down the front of the dress, accidentally revealing more cleavage.

It was a miracle I didn't rush across the room and take her right then.

She spotted me, taking in my tight black shirt and faded jeans. Her smile rose, then fell;

I knew she was wondering if she'd over dressed.

One look around the large event hall, and she'd see it was just me who'd gone casual. This was a party for my company, I could wear whatever the hell I wanted. I wasn't meeting with buyers or big wigs or anything.

Tonight, I was planning to have fun.

"Silver," she said when I got close. "Wait. Do I call you Keswick in here?"

Grinning, I scooped my arm around her middle. "It's probably better if you do."

Tucking against me, she eyeballed the milling people. "You're not acting like we're a secret."

"Because we're not. I want to make it obvious to every man in here that you're already mine."

"Then what does it matter what I call you?"

Pulling her around so that she was facing me, I was surprised to see her cocky smile. It was contagious. "Fine. Call me Silver, I'll call you Pet, and we can wonder what everyone is thinking about us."

"Alexis!" The woman who bounced our way was waving her arms frantically. In her yellow dress, her short dark hair made her look like a sunflower. I didn't need to ask her name —I knew this was Laralie.

I'd never claim I was a 'good' person. Lies came easy, especially the ones that kept you safe. Or kept others safe.

I knew everyone that was close to Alexis. I'd made it a point to research them and keep tabs. Early on, I'd justified it as a way to learn more about her... to understand her, and in that process, maybe understand why I'd become infatuated.

That hadn't worked. And so, I began sending her letters.

The dark-haired woman was still smiling, her eyes dancing between Alexis and me. "This place is beautiful!" she said, waving at the hanging lights and the long table of pastel colored snacks. "Am I crazy, or is that cake over there shaped like a giant dildo?"

Alexis patted Laralie on the shoulder, giving her a gentle shove. "No way it's—" Trailing off, she spotted the display for the first time. "What bakery *made* that thing?"

"They're a small business, but really talented. I've used them before," I said. Turning towards Laralie, I tucked on my nicest smile. "I'm guessing you're the guest who insisted on meeting me in person."

Laralie didn't even blush, she just shrugged. "I had to see if you were real."

Narrowing my eyes, I glanced at Alexis. "I'm very real."

"I'll say!" Winking, Laralie gave her friend a shove. "Okay, so, rich *and* hot?" Alexis turned beet red, but Laralie just went on. "You have any look-a-like friends you can hook me up with, Mister Very Real?"

Alexis covered her eyes, but she couldn't hide her smile. "Laralie, please."

"It's fine," I said, playing along. Spotting Florian across the room, I waved him over. "Here, this is my partner. He's a genius and *painfully* available."

Florian scoffed, acting offended as he joined our group. He was almost my height, a slim man in a pale-grey coat and black slacks. He was clearly handsome enough, because Laralie stopped goofing with Alexis, her demeanor shifting.

In seconds, she went from silly to sultry. That yellow dress caught the lights when she cocked her hip. "Hey," she said, offering a hand. "I'm Laralie, nice to meet you."

"Florian, though I guess Keswick already announced that, among other things."

Chuckling, he shook her hand. I expected him to focus on her, but his eyes danced sideways, onto Alexis. "I saw you the other day, I didn't get your name."

Recognition crossed her face. "Oh, right, you were sitting at a computer."

"I usually am," Florian said with a dramatic sigh.

Taking his hand, she squeezed. "I'm Alexis."

Florian lingered, but from the way he peered at me, I sensed he was wondering what was going on between her and I. Instead of letting him guess, I pointedly slipped my long fingers over Alexis's shoulder, cupping part of her neck possessively.

Under my touch, she shivered deliciously.

Laralie lifted her eyebrows, the first hint of her being uncomfortable. "Uh, so! Florian!

Keswick said you were a genius, what do you do?"

"I'm not a genius," he snorted.

"He is," I said. "Almost as smart as me."

Florian clutched his shirt. "Ouch." His teeth flashed, attention darting to Laralie. "I handle the oh-so-fun world of data. Well, when I'm not picking up the pieces because my *partner* has run off without any thought about his responsibilities."

Pulling Alexis closer, I kept my stare on Florian. "I think I know what my responsibility is."

"Silver," she mumbled, blushing furiously.

"Silver?" Laralie asked. Florian looked just as unsure.

Alexis rocked side to side. "It's just a nickname."

Laralie puckered her lips, but she said nothing. Sensing the tension, I nodded at

Florian. "Why don't you give Laralie a little tour around the place. She seemed interested in the dildo-cake."

Laughing, he scratched at his short, sandy hair. "The Volcano? Keswick designed that one years ago, but he refused to have it made until I found it in his backlog of files."

"Right, go show off the frosting covered version of the beast you forced my hand on."

He waved at me frantically. "For the ears of the ladies, I'll keep from making a dirty joke about your hands and forcing them onto things."

"Why else *come* to a sex toy party if it's not to hear dirty jokes?" Laralie asked.

Florian pointed at her. "I like this one."

Laralie bowed before facing Alexis. "I'll see you after, don't do anything I wouldn't do!" Together, the pair headed off towards the table of snacks. Florian bent down, speaking into her ear and causing her to laugh.

I gave Alexis a small nudge. "Would she blow off a party to get some privacy with the man she's in love with?"

She linked her fingers with mine, whispering back, "I think she would."

"Good." With long strides, I led her out the back door. "Then let's get out of here."

****

"It's so quiet," she said, stepping through the doors of Pure Pleasure. "Do you not have any security—ah!" A small, sharp beep had surprised her.

Grinning, I pulled the doors shut behind us. From my pocket, I slid out my phone to show her the screen. "This is my security. It's an app Florian and I created."

She leaned close, watching the phone. There was a live feed of where we stood, and she looked up, trying to locate the camera. "How does it work?"

"Motion sensors. They feed into my phone, alerting me if there's anyone moving around in here after I set the alarm."

"Huh. That's clever."

"Don't flatter me *too* hard," I teased. Scooping up her hand, I marveled at how I'd never get bored of that instant tingle. "This way. I want to show you something."

We walked through a side-hall, the darkness thick around us. I didn't need any light to know where I was going; I'd walked these floors for thousands of hours. I knew my building like the back of my hand. The only one who might know it as well was Florian.

It was his idea to make a display room of our most popular toys, too.

"Oh my gosh," Alexis laughed when I flicked on the overhead lamps. The room was wide, long tables of flat metal and glass along the walls. On top of each of them sat an array of multi-colored sex toys.

She pulled away from me, wandering the room with amazement strong on her face. "If I'd seen this room first, the dildo-cake wouldn't have shocked me."

Following her, I trailed wherever her eyes paused. I wanted to see into her head, eager to know what she thought about each item. "It's mostly to show to investors, or the occasional curious visitor."

Her hand went up, hovering just above the curved tip of a silver, modern-art styled toy. "This one is kind of pretty. Did you really design *all* of these?" She was acting amused, but her blush was creeping up her throat.

"Most."

"Can I ask why?"

Alexis had stopped moving, her attention fixing on me. There was an undeniable eroticness to how she was standing, fingers just inches from the surface of something I'd designed to make women come again and again.

Swaying closer to her, I stood on the other side of the display case. "Because I'm obsessed with the idea of knowing I'm the reason girls are squirming in bed. But honestly, it's because it makes me a lot of money."

A ripple moved over her brow. "That's all?"

Reaching across, I plucked the toy from the table. It was heavy, most of that coming from the sharp metal base meant to keep it pointing upright. "Did I need another reason?"

She half-turned away from me. "Saying it bluntly makes you sound heartless."

I found myself staring helplessly at the curve of her ear. It was bare, empty, and I hated that. "Pet, I'm not heartless. My heart has plenty of room in it for you, and it has nothing to do with wanting to keep my bank accounts flush."

Looking at the floor, then me, she sighed. "You're right. I was just hoping you had another reason for creating stuff. When I was..." Trailing off, she shook her head. "Never mind."

"No, tell me."

Her black pupils sucked up all the green in her eyes. "When I was planning to leave and go out to LA, I was—it'll sound so stupid." At her waist, she twisted her fingers together. "I had these big dreams of getting accepted into a college for designing clothes. That was what I wanted to do. Remember the dress you saw me in five years ago?"

My heart dehydrated, shrinking. "You made that?"

She didn't answer with her words, but I knew.

Tension turned my muscles into useless rocks. They crumbled, cracked, threatening to crush everything inside of me that I dared to call human. I'd already accepted that I'd have to spend an eternity making up for my sins... for what I'd done to this woman.

Was there no end to the destruction my revenge had created?

Breathing heavily, I said, "Tell me you didn't stop creating clothing." *Say it wasn't because of me.*

There were no tears on her cheeks, but her smile was just as tragic. "I'm a secretary now at a fashion magazine, it's pretty close to what I wanted to do. And it keeps my accounts flush, like you said." Alexis laughed, like she wanted to ease the mood, but the noise was as dangerous as broken glass. "I probably wouldn't have made it as a designer. Anyway, forget it. That was a lifetime ago."

I ruined everything for her.

Everything.

"I think Laralie is texting me." Taking her phone from her purse, she glanced at me and froze. "Silver?" She was staring at the toy in my grip; it was shaking from how hard I squeezed. "Are you okay?"

Carefully, I set the heavy object back on the display. Alexis couldn't have known what was going on in my skull, yet her eyes burned warily on me. I'd be stupid to think I could hide how her story had affected me.

Hiding isn't the answer.

"I'll fix it," I whispered.

"What? What did you say?"

Lifting my eyes, I saw how she watched me. Alexis... my Pet... she held such concern for me, the man who'd broken her future into chunks and then swallowed them up.

I'd spend every fucking second of my life making it up to her.

"Silver, what is it?" she asked. "If it's about what I said, forget it. I was being dramatic, I—"

"No. I won't forget it." Faster than lightning I crossed around the table, capturing her shoulders. It was easy to pull her against me, her purple dress sliding over my shirt. "The last thing I'll ever do is forget."

"Wha—ah!"

Scooping her up, I ran from the room. She clung to me, nails cutting in deliciously. Ignoring her baffled shouts, I carried her quickly up to my office. The door was locked—I always locked it after hours. In seconds, I yanked my keys out, working the lock free.

The door bounced off the wall, and then, she bounced off the couch in my corner where I dropped her. "What are you doing?" she blurted.

Kneeling beside her, I pushed her purse and phone from her hands. They tumbled to the floor, forgotten. Alexis sat up, her mouth open in surprise. That made it easy to steal a long kiss.

And another.

And then another.

In that room lit only by the city lights through the window, we clung to each other and said no words. I didn't need them, and she certainly didn't. I knew this woman inside and out, but still, she revealed a new scar to me every time we were together.

Was it twisted that I wanted to take that pain from her with pleasure?

Her body slid over the leather couch, thighs spreading for me before I touched her anywhere but her lips. Taking the hint, I hooked her dress up, revealing another set of the beautiful lingerie I'd bought her.

Honestly, she'd have looked just as magnificent with nothing on.

"Is this okay?" she asked, breaking away. "Having sex in your office?"

"It's *my* office. Of course it's fucking okay." Ripping her panties down, I felt the texture of the thigh-highs she'd squeezed into. "Unless you want me to stop?"

Her eyes were wild, frenzied. "Don't you dare."

Smiling wide, I buried my face in her cunt and inhaled. *Fucking hell.* Grazing my thumb over her clit, I pulled her lips further apart to expose it. The pink glint called to me, what could I do but answer?

"Ah!" she whimpered, clawing at my hair. Her pussy ground on my face, wetness slicking my cheeks. Two fingers trailed up her slit, teasing until her thighs shook around my ears.

I wasn't so cruel, though.

Inch by inch, I happily gave her what she wanted.

Alexis groaned, arching while my fingers filled her. Bending them, I pet the roof of her tunnel, exploring her vigorously. I wasn't expecting her to shiver, tensing around my knuckles in an abrupt orgasm.

It shocked us both, my cock raging in my pants angrily. "That's it," I growled. "That's too much for me." My belt clanked down, jeans draping low enough to free my swollen prick.

Her hand found me, circling my base tight. "You're so hard," she said in wonder. "Fuck me, please, hurry and fuck me."

My eyes fluttered in my skull. The sensation of her touch was making me dizzy, but it was her insatiable hunger that had my lower belly tingling. We hadn't used a condom last time, so I didn't bother looking for one now.

Hooking her ankles, I shoved her down on the couch until she bent in half. Her pussy was spread wide, my cock sliding up and down

398

along her entrance. The fat tip bumped her clit, causing her to tremble. "You want this?" I asked.

She nodded, her red lips parting in a silent cry.

Biting my tongue, I sank into her in one fast, solid thrust. Alexis cried out, nails scraping over my lower back. We stayed like that for a full minute, my eyes leveling on hers. She asked, "What are you doing?"

Squeezing her ass, I smirked. "Fuck yourself on me. Grind until you get off."

In frustration, she wriggled as much as she could. My weight was holding her down; only her clit was rubbing me with how I'd angled myself. "I can't!" she said, her brow furrowing. "Just fuck me, don't play any games."

"I love games, though." When she went to push me away, I held her tighter. She was pinned, my cock stretching her out while her clit could only get any contact if she gyrated with all her might.

Breathing faster, she realized I was serious.

Swallowing, she closed her eyes and started to rock. It was barely an inch, allowing her to just graze her twitching clit on my flat stomach. Her cunt rippled, strangling me as it heated up in desperation.

There's nothing sexier than a woman who'll do anything to come.

"Good," I whispered, licking her firm nipples. Her moan sent tremors to my core. At this rate, she was going to get me off before she reached the peak herself. But I had a few tricks up my sleeve.

Licking my fingers, I winked at her. Reaching behind us, I trailed a fingertip along her inner thigh. At the cleft of her ass, I rubbed her asshole—every muscle in her body locked up.

"Oh fuck," she whimpered. I was amazed she didn't question what I was doing. She must have been too turned on to care, her need to orgasm too great.

Slippery heat embraced my painfully erect cock. Alexis moaned, turning her face away from me. I could feel the electric current in her pussy, it traveled through and into my flexing shaft. She was right on the edge, so close to coming.

Burying my finger deep in her ass, I bent my spine into a perfect C and sat up. Her pussy milked me, her asshole thrumming on my knuckle. Together we came, our cells waking with the hyper-awareness of orgasm.

Even when I was done filling her with my seed, she *still* writhed. And I *still* shivered with the pressure of release. I'd never felt anything so good, the pleasure rolling on to my toes and beyond.

Pulling my hand from her, I breathed out sharply. "What the hell was that?" I asked out loud.

There were stars in her eyes, the pink of roses on her lips. If you could bottle contentment and joy, drink it till you drowned, you still wouldn't have matched the emotion on her face.

Alexis was in love.

This was love.

I'd known it—or I'd thought I had. Until just then, I'd never actually experienced the extent of our compassion. This desire for each other, it might just kill us. And would that even be a tragedy?

She pulled me to her, kissing me gently. "I love you, do you know that?"

I smiled around her lips. "You've said it before."

"But do you *know*."

I almost said, "Yes." Then I stopped, weighing my words. "You really mean it. Even after what I've done to you, you're able to love me?"

Her hand trailed down the back of my neck. "I didn't realize I was living a half-life until you showed up. I don't know anyone I could ever love *except* for you."

The support of our bodies paled next to what our souls could offer. We stayed like that on my couch, long after the party had ended... but I wanted forever.

Alexis broke the silence; I'd thought she'd fallen asleep. "I want to ask you something, and you have to answer it."

"I can't hear the question first?" She looked me in the eye, pure seriousness. "Alright. Ask me."

Trailing her palm down my chest, she lowered her voice. "Why did you rob Old Stone bank? You mentioned... revenge."

She was lying on top of my heart, she could feel it drumming. "It's not something you want to hear."

"Of course I do. Anything that let's me understand you better is worth knowing."

Tracing the line of her cheek, I hesitated. "It's a sad story, and I'm terrified of making you sad ever again."

Light entered her eyes, turning the green color into a summer pond. I could see to the bottom, her emotions swimming like fish. Leaning up, she met my lips with a tender kiss. "If I cry, you'll just have to hold me. Is that so bad?"

Cradling her against me, I luxuriated in her skin on mine. "No. Not at all."

It was a story I'd never told another soul.

I had never planned to.

Lying there under the weight of the most perfect woman in the world, I tore back the layers of my past.

And I told her everything.

"How long does he have to live?"

I asked the question, but the answer couldn't get through the cotton in my brain. Cancer. How could my younger brother have cancer? He was too young, too healthy, too...

Too innocent.

"Mr. Silverwell? Mr. Silverwell." I was only nineteen, I wasn't used to being called a Mr. Anything. "Keswick." The doctor said my name sharply, pulling me from my funk. When he saw I was listening, he sighed. "I know this is hard. But, if he does the treatment exactly as planned, he might live longer than anyone could hope for."

He was wrong, of course.

I was already hoping for eternity.

"As his guardian," he said, flipping through his paperwork, "You'll get to make the call. But you should really talk to him first."

Of course I would talk to him. I'd also do my fucking best to convince him that he had to do this. He was fifteen, how could he NOT fight? I was practicing every argument I could think of when I sat across from Brodie in our apartment.

He beat me to it.

"I want to live," he said, no hint of fear or wavering. "I'll do whatever I have to. Give me chemo, give me prayer, give me anything." Looking me in the eye, he smiled so that his dimples showed. "What's the point of living if you aren't willing to risk everything to keep doing it?"

I'd never hugged him harder than that moment.

We had such belief in our own strength... in the good of the world. How could we possibly lose?

The insurance company told us how.

"It's the policy," the third man on the phone said to me. "Your parents are the ones that put you on this plan, and you've never changed it. It doesn't pay for the kind of treatment you're seeking. I'm sorry, Mr. Silverwell."

"This isn't about any fucking policy!" I screamed. "You're talking about someone's life! Doesn't that matter at all!?"

"Sir, if you like, I can put you through to customer service—"

"Fuck your customer service!"

The man on the line went quiet. "...Listen. There's nothing we can do for you."

"Can, or won't?" I spat.

"Won't," he admitted, and I sensed bitter humor in his tone. "Good luck, Sir." He

probably hung up, but I couldn't say, because I'd dropped the phone onto the floor and stomped it to pieces.

Nothing about this made sense to me. How could we live in a world where a boy—a BOY—could die because an insurance company decided their 'policy' didn't cover treatment? How was this possible?

Worse, they'd been siphoning money from us the whole time. Each bill claimed different things, saying the basic procedures Brodie was undergoing weren't covered, either.

In a single month, we went from two happy brothers... to two people crushed under massive debt. But screw the money, I wanted my brother to get the treatment he needed. Even if it could only give him a little more time, it would be enough.

Anything would be enough.

I'd been working as a coder at a security software company since before graduating. Even as a tiny child, I'd been fascinated with computers. It came naturally to me. I pushed my company for more hours, for advances in my salary.

It didn't matter. None of it did.

Brodie passed away four months after being diagnosed. And still, the insurance company wasn't done kicking us into the mud. They held his life policy, and they decided that his death was preventable.

Preventable with the treatment they refused to provide.

I was broke. Not just financially... but emotionally. It was a hateful numbness I'd never experienced, or dreamed was possible. How could humans feel like I did? But then, how could they feel so little that they'd let a young boy wither and die?

I didn't want answers.

I wanted to punish them.

It's unsettling how easy it was to find out which bank Crodan Insurance kept their money in. It was even easier to figure out how to crack into Old Stone's system. I'd need to plug the coder-chip into their system on site, but that was fine.

That day, I'd taken out the gun my father had left behind. It was one of the only things my parents had left for us before they'd died. I didn't think about what I was doing, as far as what happened to me. My family was all dead. If I got my revenge, I'd be satisfied.

But when I was prepping to leave... I couldn't bring myself to load the gun.

I couldn't let anyone else get hurt.

An empty gun is still a good threat, though. I just had to keep it secret that it was free of bullets.

Inside the bank, I was cold. Calm. Everyone around me was muted and grey and

410

faceless. Any of them would have worked as a hostage.

Then I saw you.

You were standing there in this flowing dress, the only source of color in the whole room... the whole world. The second you looked into my eyes, I knew I had to act. If I didn't, I'd think about the risk... the danger... and I'd back out.

So I grabbed you.

And you know the rest.

I paused the story, transfixed by how her wide eyes were glistening. Unshed tears had gathered; I wiped them away before they could wet her cheeks. She bent away, rubbing her eyes vigorously. "I knew you stole from the insurance company. I didn't know..." Trailing off, she covered her mouth.

Hugging her, I set my chin on the top of her head. "Shh, it's alright."

She sniffled, speaking before I was ready. "How did you get away?"

My lashes brushed my skin, I saw the darkness behind my eyelids. "I pulled off my mask and merged into the panicked crowd I'd created. It wasn't hard to slip away. I told you, I had no intention of staying here once I was done. I planned to leave the city... I did that."

And then you drew me back.

Florian had been confused by my decision to bring our company here. When I'd met him in San Francisco, he'd been working at a start-up; the one Gerard owned. We'd been the most talented pair there, so we'd hit it off.

Perhaps that was why he'd trusted my decision to quit and begin again.

If I was as smart as him, I had to have a good reason.

He'd never have guessed Alexis was my reason.

- Chapter Twenty-five -
Alexis

Where is it? I wondered, throwing my blanket off of my bed. Other than my wrinkled sheets, nothing stared back at me. *Where could I have left it?*

Tracing my steps, I worked to remember the last place I'd had my phone.

Last night was the party... and I had it when I... Stopping in my tracks, I slapped my own forehead. "Dammit," I said out loud. "I left it in his office!" It had fallen from my hands on the couch, but when I'd left, I'd only grabbed my purse.

Groaning, I hurried to get changed. *I'll swing by after work.* The idea of going the whole day without talking to him was draining my mood. I'd gotten so used to our contact.

This distance reminded me of when I'd first cut off his gifts.

Laralie spent most of the day gabbing to me about how much she liked Florian. She said he was a genius, funny, and probably as rich as Keswick.

It was hard not to smile at her enthusiasm. I even had an excuse when she accused me of ignoring her texts. "I lost my phone," I said, dodging her lightly-tossed paperclips.

"Uh huh. Right." Flicking another clip, she grinned. "Let's go on a double date, how about it?"

"That would be fun." Thinking about how Silver might not curb his behavior in public with me, I shifted on my seat. "Let me think it over." Eyeing the clock, I grabbed my coat and purse. "I've got to go."

Laralie spun in her chair. "Meeting him, are you?" When I flapped my hands, she just giggled. "Ask him about the date!"

"Of course, right." Ducking into the elevator, I jogged to where I'd parked my car. *It's past five, will he still be there?* What if I missed him? I hadn't memorized his phone number, at this rate, I'd have to go straight to his condo and drag him back to his office.

Starting my car, the radio flicked on. It was still on a news station, and they were going on about another bank being robbed. *That hacker is still out there.* Eyeing the radio, I frowned nervously. *I hope they catch him soon.* I hadn't heard from Vermont in forever, it had become easy to forget about the robberies at all.

My tires squeaked when I pulled up along the sidewalk outside of Pure Pleasure. Two figures were standing near the entrance, every window glinting like obsidian. *Am I too late, did they close up?*

Nearly dropping my car keys, I stumbled out the door. One of the men laughed, his sharp cheekbones casting hard shadows on his face. Florian was easy to recognize, but Silver was even easier.

"Hey!" I shouted, waving my arms. I jogged up the steps to meet them.

Silver turned my way, pleasantly surprised by my sudden appearance. "What are you doing here?"

Catching my breath, I pointed at the doors. "Did you lock everything up already?"

He shot a look at the building. "I did."

"Dammit." Straightening up, I fixed my wind-tossed hair. "I'm sorry to ask you to do this, but can you let me in? I left my phone in your office last night."

Florian gave me a meaningful look. "Oho."

"Don't tease," I mumbled. "I feel bad enough about it."

Silver reached for his pocket. "Relax. It's not a problem." He was halfway to sticking the key in the lock when the sound of tires cut through the air. The white, beaten up Subaru that skid into place behind my car was one I recognized. Even so, I had to look twice to convince myself it was Vermont.

He shut the car door loudly, eyes fixing on me—then Silver. A weight settled in my belly, my muscles going sluggish. "Why is he here?" I asked softly.

Silver flicked his attention to me. The detective's voice drew him back. "Keswick Silverwell?" he asked, one hand under his coat.

Lifting his chin, Silver studied the man like he was a piece of rotten food. "Do you need something?"

In one fast motion, Vermont hooked his body against Silver's. I screamed, covering my mouth in surprise. His face was shoved violently against the building. To his credit, Silver didn't even grunt in pain.

"What are you doing?" I shouted, starting to run forward. Sirens and flashing lights descended upon our once quiet corner of the city. Florian threw his head side to side, his skin both yellow and shiny. He was as terrified and confused as I was.

Detective Roose jammed his forearm onto the back of Silver's neck. "You're under arrest for the hackings at Old Stone Bank, Goldman and Wellmont."

I'd known that this was coming. How could we arrive at anything else? Silver had always been a fugitive.

I was a fool to think our pasts wouldn't matter.

Police officers stormed us, circling to help Vermont handcuff Silver. Florian stumbled out of the way, his hands in front of him like he expected to be arrested, too.

Running on pure instinct, I jumped forward. "What are you doing to him!?"

Amber irises focused on me, Silver's face a torrent of rage and defeat. His pain was *my* pain; I reached out, but one of the three officers pushed me away. "Stop this, please!" I shouted.

Vermont yanked Silver's arms back, holding them and forcing him down the steps towards his Subaru. He was ignoring me. *Me*, the girl he'd hoped would be the key to finding the man he was after.

Unwillingly, I'd been exactly that.

Struggling against the cop, I yelled at the back of Vermont's head. "Listen to me, he didn't do it! *Listen!*" I filled my chest. "*Vermont!*"

The detective locked up, his shoulders stiffening. Without a hint of gentleness, he pushed Silver into the back of his car. The door slammed, then he swung his stare at me, climbing the steps.

Encouraged by his approach, I said, "He didn't do it! Silver is innocent!"

"Silver?" Vermont asked. His nose wrinkled. "Is that your pet name for him?"

My heart went cold. "Vermont..."

Scowling, he took the pen from behind his ear, twisting it. "That's why you were protecting him, right? How long did you know?"

Wordlessly, I shook my head. *No no no.* I stopped shoving against the officer, my body going limp. "Vermont, please. He didn't do it."

"It's *Detective Roose.*" Spinning, he cut his hand through the air. The cop released me, backing away.

Through the window of the car, I saw Silver watching. The sight of him gave me strength. "He's innocent, you have to believe me!"

"*Believe* you?" I'd never seen Vermont so furious. "You lied to me over and over, Alexis. In what fucking world would I ever believe you again?"

One by one, the officers climbed into their cars. Roose ripped his driver's side door open. Over the roof, those once-friendly brown eyes locked on me. "I really thought you were on my side."

Sides? I thought desperately. *This isn't about sides!* This was about grey areas... about helping the people you loved!

Shaking himself, Roose ducked into his car. Like a series of missiles the cops and him flew down the road. Silver watched me until he was gone.

This isn't happening. But it was. It fucking was.

Just when I'd gotten my life back, it had all turned to dust in my hands. Clenching my fists, I shivered under the assault of the cool evening air. *What do I do now?*

Florian was still standing beside me, as shocked by his boss being arrested as me. His face was pale, his eyes far away.

"He didn't do it," I said softly.

He blinked owlishly at me. "How are you so sure?"

"I just am."

My sincerity gave him pause. Nodding slightly, he tucked his hands in his pockets. "He's a good guy, but that doesn't matter. The government always has its cocks up our asses, even if we're innocent. If there's any justice, Kes will beat this."

Something chipped at the back of my memory. "Right," I said slowly. "He'll beat this."

Checking his watch, Florian winced. "I should go back in there," he said, pointing towards Pure Pleasure. "I mean, in case the cops get a warrant and decide to tear apart everything. People could lose their jobs after this. Fuck, I had a shit ton to do *before* we lost our head-honcho."

"Wait," I said. "What should *I* do?"

"You?" He was already walking backwards. "I don't know. I guess go down to the station, or maybe call up a lawyer for him. That's what I'd want if I was arrested." He offered a sympathetic smile. "Good luck, and see you around."

A lawyer, that's smart. "Bye," I said, not noticing he was too far away to hear me. Silver was going to need someone to defend him. He was innocent—sort of—and a good lawyer could prove that!

Tapping my cheek, I came close to smiling. *Yeah, that's it. I just have to...* Patting my pockets, then my purse, my heart dropped. *My phone!* That was why I'd come back here in the first place!

Facing the building, I jumped the steps two at a time. The doors were dark, I'd seen Silver shutting everything down earlier when I'd shown up. I thrilled with relief to find the entrance unlocked from Florian going back in.

The alarm beeped behind me. *Motion sensors, right.* Silver had shown me how it all worked. Of course, he wouldn't be looking at his phone right now. Or maybe ever again.

In the eerie waiting room, the water cooler bubbled in near darkness. A reddish light by the hallway was the only illumination I had. When I entered the room full of computers, they were all glowing blue. Shielding my eyes, I lifted my chin. There was a rattling sound, wood banging over and over. "Florian?" I asked, spotting him at the top of the stairs to Silver's office.

He spun, his eyes flashing like a raccoon's in the dark. "What are you doing back here?" he asked me, wiping his face.

"My phone," I said, climbing the steps to join him. "It's still in his office. I really need it."

"Well, good fucking luck," he groaned. "The door's locked, and Keswick has the only key."

The grip of depression started to strangle me. It didn't get far before I remembered what Silver had given me two weeks back. Unzipping my purse, I slid out the spare keys. "One of these might work." *He said he'd never let me think I couldn't reach him.*

The memory of his promise cut through me.

Florian's eyebrows flew to the top of his scalp. "Thank fucking goodness! I didn't know what I was going to do."

It took a few seconds, but one of the keys clicked perfectly in the lock. Jiggling the door open, I flicked on the nearest lamp. "What were you trying to get in here for?" I asked, scanning the rug frantically. "Paperwork or something?"

Florian ignored me, dropping into Silver's chair. The computer 'beeped' on, his fingers flying over the keyboard.

Crouching, I spotted my cellphone under the couch in the corner. The weight of it in my hand was a relief. Turning it on, I scanned the messages Silver had sent me overnight.

Silver: There's so much I want to tell you.

Silver: So much I want to do with you.

Silver: I want forever.

Silver: I love you, Pet.

Each of them cemented my desire to free him. Living without that man felt impossible.

"Alright," I said, standing to acknowledge Florian. "I'm going. I need to get to the police station right away."

He looked up at me briefly. "Yeah, yeah. I've gotta finish some stuff real quick. Say hello to the government cocks for me."

He'd said that earlier, too. Was that why it was familiar? *No,* I told myself. *I've heard that before, but when?*

Rounding the desk, I meant to ask him where he'd heard that phrase. The brightness of the computer screen drew me in like a moth. Several pop-ups were open, numbers flying as fast as Florian's fingers. What looked like timers were counting down. "What the fuck?" I whispered automatically. "What are you *doing?*"

He glanced at me, then away. "Nothing, work stuff. Go help Keswick."

In a black box, white code tumbled by in a waterfall of gibberish. I knew exactly where I'd seen that all before.

Silver spoons for some, government cocks for everyone else.

Cupping a hand over my mouth, I bit back a shout. *Detective Roose!* He'd shown me that phrase mixed in with some cryptic computer vomit in our first interview. He'd called it the hacker's calling card, he...

Florian glanced at me, his fingers pausing on the keys. My horrified face must have given me away. "Shit," he said.

Backing up a step, I lifted my hands in front of me. "It was you!" Ripping my phone out, I went to dial for help.

Florian jumped up in a panic, knocking my phone away from me. "Shit," he said again, his hands up in the air like mine. We must have looked ridiculous.

I moved first, scrambling to get the phone where it had fallen. Florian was all arms, wrapping me up, his palm pushing my cheek to the rug. "Let me go!" I shouted, struggling madly. The phone was inches away from me. *I have to call the cops!*

"No one was supposed to find out!" Breathing heavily, he sat on my back. His knee stabbed between my shoulder blades painfully. "Fuck, fuck! Just stay down, I need to stop this!"

Stop what, stop me? I didn't know what he was talking about, but I wasn't going to stay down. I reached back and dug my nails into his ankle. His scream was satisfying.

Florian rocked off of me, enough that I could give myself rug burn as I crawled forward. I grabbed for my phone; Florian shoved me with everything he had, my chest bouncing off of the floor.

The wind was kicked out of me, I gaped soundlessly as I rolled on my side. Panting, he stood over me and kicked my phone into the far corner by the door. Coiling his fingers in my hair, he wrenched me back. My scream was a mere whine, I could barely breathe.

Twisting me into a choke-hold with one arm, Florian yanked me towards the desk. This new angle let me see the screen again. One of the timers was blinking, a red warning that said 'two minutes.'

"Dammit!" he shouted, dropping me on the floor. I hunched there, working to fill my lungs, my gasps ragged. Over my head, I heard him tapping on the keyboard. "Gotta stop it, gotta, fuuuck."

The timer, I realized through my daze. *He's worried about the timer.* I didn't know why, but if he was scared of it going off, then I wanted it to happen.

His scrawny legs hung over me. Bunching my muscles, I pulled my knees to my stomach and then kicked them out. Florian toppled, slipping against the rolling chair as he collapsed to the rug. "Augh!" he shouted.

Dizzy, I grabbed the desk's ledge, using it to stand. My phone looked miles away, but I took it step by step. Behind me, he snarled a nonsense sentence of swears and hatred.

Move, get the phone!

One leg gave out, but I landed in arm's length. Snatching my cell, I frantically dialed, rolling to watch Florian looming over me. He was an avalanche, and I had a few mere seconds to speak.

Vermont picked up instantly, his voice clipped. "What now, Alexis? I'm on my way—"

"It wasn't him!"

"Huh? What are you talking about?"

Leaning into the phone, I started to shriek. "It's not Silver—not Keswick! It was Florian!"

"Who the hell is Florian?"

The hacker cracked his fist into my ear. Every color in existence spun in my vision, and I noticed I was looking up at the ceiling.

"You little bitch!" Dropping the phone, he crushed it under his heel. "You really wanted to ruin everything, didn't you?"

The computer made a tiny clicking sound. Florian froze where he was, his face turning ghostly white. I knew that noise was a *good* noise.

Whirling, he ran for the desk. Slamming his palms on either side of the keyboard, he boggled at the screen. The blue light made his face alien. "No! No no no!" Pounding the keys, he scraped his nails over his temples. I'd never seen a person so unhinged.

I did it, the timer went off.

His stare flicked to me, and my joy melted.

"I hope it was worth it." He stalked towards me around the desk. "Ruining my alibi is the last thing you'll do on this damn Earth."

Once, five years ago, I'd known the fear of death. It had clung to me the moment Silver had put a gun to my head. Watching Florian approach should have locked me down like that first time.

But I wasn't that girl anymore.

Instead of crumbling into a shaking pile, I forced myself to run for the door. He was breathing down my neck. Wind grazed my elbow; he'd moved to catch me.

I was already bolting down the stairs.

"Get back here!" he screamed behind me.

Taking a hard turn, I plowed around a corner. The throbbing in my head was making me ill. When I burst into a room full of brightly colored sex toys on display, dread became my new companion. This was where I'd been with Silver last night. It wasn't the exit.

In my panic, I'd taken a wrong turn.

His shoes stampeded behind me on the hard floor. Low grunts made him sound like a dragon that planned to eat me alive. I didn't know the full weight of what I'd done to Florian, but he was furious. Deadly.

With a final growl, he shoved into me before I could run again. Toppling against the table, I sent vibrators and other items crumbling to the floor around me.

This is it, I thought in wonder. *This is how I die.*

My eyes blurred, focusing on the texture of the tiles in front of me. The scuffling shoes of my attacker approached, echoing like thunder claps. *I can't give up.* What a strong, useless thought. I was fighting tooth and nail, and still, Florian had broken me down.

But I wasn't done.

Not yet.

"I'll kill you," he huffed, finger-tips digging into my shoulder. "I never planned to hurt anyone, but fuck if you haven't changed that, you dumb bitch."

Spinning, I swung at his temple with the full strength of every bad thing that had ever happened to me behind it. The edge of the heavy metal base on the toy cut into his skin, colliding off of his skull.

Florian toppled to the ground in a giant heap.

Breathing in great swallows of air, I stared down at him savagely. My grip on the big red dildo was bone-white. I'd done it. I'd actually done it. For the first time in my life, I'd faced down someone trying to hurt me...

And I'd *won*.

"Here," I mumbled, tossing the toy so that it bounced off of his temple. "Have one of those cocks you won't shut up about."

"Alexis!"

Whipping my eyes up, I stared in disbelief. The man I loved, his hands bound by metal cuffs, was coming my way in a hurry. Did I have a concussion?

"Silver?" I asked, swaying on my feet.

Impossibly fast he crossed the room, catching me in spite of his bound hands. "Pet!" he growled, cradling me where he knelt. "Are you alright?"

Blinking, I reached up to touch his cheek. "How are you here?"

Pushing his hips to my forehead, he embraced me furiously. "You can thank your friend over there for that."

Vermont approached Florian. Another pair of officers entered the room, bending over the fallen man. Their loud chattering said his injuries were mild. I'd hit him as hard as I could, but he wasn't in critical health.

Sensing my stare, Vermont looked at me. His ears were glowing red; the pen was tugged free, waving between his knuckles. "Your guy there wouldn't shut the hell up about us turning around once he heard you on the phone with me. I thought he was going to smash his face through the damn window just to get here."

My chin swung like a pendulum. "How did you know where I was?"

"You tripped the alarm," Silver said. "I heard it go off in my pocket." Briefly, he glared at the detective. "I told him something was wrong, to check my phone and see the cameras, but he ignored me."

Vermont shrugged uncomfortably. "I thought he was looking for a way out."

From the corner of my vision, I saw them cuffing Florian and pulling him to his feet. He was groggy, his head lolling. Still watching him, I spoke softly to Silver. "You got here so fast."

He cupped my cheeks, tenderly feeling the swelling above my eye. "We were still on the road when we turned around."

Vermont crouched beside Silver, reaching for his wrists. "Let me get these off, they're pointless now." The cuffs slid free, and while I saw his skin was raw from struggling, Silver didn't bother checking out his injuries. He was too busy fixating on mine.

"He could have killed you," Silver whispered hotly. His hands held me tighter, there was a good chance he'd never let me go. "Why would you put yourself in danger like that for me?"

I ran the pad of my thumb across his brow, then down to the dip of his cheekbone. "When you're in love, you stop caring about the risks."

Silver looked down at me with his mouth fixed in a perfect line. I had a minute of feeling ridiculous. Had I *really* said that?

Burying my worries with his lips, the man I loved... the man I trusted... kissed me until I knew nothing but that moment. There was no pain, no fear, no torment. All that existed was the two of us wrapped together.

What more could I ever need?

- Epilogue -

Silver

The next few days were a funny blur.

Florian was, of course, charged with hacking the security systems of all the banks. Even Old Stone, a crime that belonged entirely to me. I didn't mind; it meant I could finally stop looking over my shoulder.

It was hard to feel sympathy for my old friend. He'd intended to let me take the fall for every robbery. The automatic system he'd buried in my computer was set on a timer. It would hack each bank one by one, tucking the money safely away in encrypted bits in overseas accounts.

Every bit of evidence would point to me.

But then, I'd been arrested before he'd expected me to be. And the next timer was too soon, if it went off, it would make it harder to prove I'd done everything—because I was in cuffs at the time.

He probably could have said *I'd* been using an auto-timed system, but his fingers were all over the code, the damn calling card. He'd been too cocky... he always had been.

At some point, he'd found the old code I'd used years ago to hack Old Stone. I think it must have been around the time he'd found some old designs of mine, or perhaps that had all been a ploy to dig through my files. It didn't matter.

He'd found the trail of my actions, and then he'd refined my program. I always said he was a genius. He was also dead to me.

I'd never forgive anyone that hurt Alexis.

And that was why I had no qualms handing all the evidence on my computer over to Detective Roose. And why I had no problem tweaking the code to remove any hint that I'd ever touched it in the past.

Florian could have all the credit.

I just wanted her.

****

"Now, don't be too impressed," she said, setting the casserole dish on the table between us. "I make a pretty good macaroni and cheese bake. Not bragging."

Chuckling, I folded my hands in front of me. It was the first time Alexis had let me into her home, a fact I'd brought up to her several times. Apparently, after being exposed to my own place, she'd been too nervous to show me where she lived.

How could she not realize that anyplace she was, was worth more than the most luxurious house in existence?

Waving steam away with an oven mitt, she beamed. "Look good?"

Squinting at the bright orange cheesy pile, I smiled. "Smells good."

"Then dig in!"

We ate with occasional laughter, and the occasional fidgeting on her part. I had no control when it came to touching her leg under the table. When our plates were cleared, she poured us some wine.

Sipping the tangy drink, I nodded at her. "Thanks for making us dinner."

"Oh, it was nothing." She squeezed the glass tight. "I still don't know why you were so insistent on coming here. Wouldn't dinner at a fancy restaurant be nicer?"

"Maybe," I said, feeling inside my pocket. "But I suspect you'd prefer privacy?"

Alexis crinkled her mouth. "For what?"

Gently, I slid the soft, black box across the table. It bumped her elbow, she nearly spilled her drink as she sat back in surprise.

"What's this?" she asked, her palm cradling the box.

My smile was sly.

Setting her wine aside, she carefully opened it. Her eyes flashed between the gift, then me, then back again. "How?"

I was overjoyed with her reaction. "I don't think the pawn shop owner was expecting to sell those to someone just an hour after he'd bought them."

Alexis lifted the earrings, the emerald depths stretching for miles in the light. Twisting them, she touched the silver edges in wonderment. "I didn't think I'd ever see them again."

I didn't mention that I was glad she didn't throw them away when the post office worker tried to give them to her. I'd had to go retrieve the gift from him myself.

Curling my fingers around her wrist, I urged her closer. One by one, I clipped the earrings into place onto the perfect shells of her ears.

"How do they look?" she asked, cupping one.

"Much nicer than they did in a glass case."

The fringe of her smile started to fade. "You hung onto these for weeks, why give them to me now?"

"Well," I said, bending my knee to the floor. My insides flipped with how wide her eyes became, and the "o" shape of her mouth flushed me with desire. "I wanted to make sure that they matched perfectly with this."

Withdrawing the ring from my pocket, I held it between us. The silver metal glinted, green emeralds made nearly black by the clarity of the diamond between them.

"Silver..." She whispered my name like a prayer.

Taking her left hand, I teased my fingers over her palm. "Marry me, Alexis. Come with me to LA and let me give you the life I stole. You wanted the big city dream, you wanted to explore your career and find who you were. Do that with me a your side. With me... as your husband."

Alexis—my beautiful woman, my perfect pet—jumped to her feet. The chair fell over, clattering on her scuffed kitchen floors. My heart sank into the deepest part of my being. *Is she going to say no?*

Her whole arm trembled when she lifted it. I still held the ring, but I thought she was imagining it on her bare finger. "What about your company here?"

"I can find someone to run it. I said before, I own others. I'll even open a new one in Los Angeles, you can design outfits for it— whatever you want."

"And you think that will help me find out who I really am?"

Fuck, I could feel my pulse all the way in my throat. "I do. And if not, I'll find out what will, and give you that."

"Stop," she said firmly. Leveling her eyes on me, she blinked as if she'd never seen me before. "Marriage, a dream career I gave up on forever ago? You don't need to do any of that for me. I might have missed out on the life I'd planned... but I already know who I am."

Leaning closer, I stared up at her. "Then tell me."

Alexis collapsed forward, a force that was soft as spring wind and as solid as an oak tree. Cradling my jaw, she pressed her nose to mine. "I'm yours," she whispered. "That's plenty enough for me."

Shutting my eyes, I breathed inward. *She's mine. Forever mine.*

"But," she said, glancing down at the ring I held. "If it's no difference to you, I think I could handle being your wife, too."

Grinning, I thumbed her chin and made her look at me. "Is that a yes?"

She held out her hand, energy coming off of her in droves. It fueled me, my skin burning as I slid the ring into place. When it settled, we both gasped from the sudden burst of sharp static.

In a daze, she asked, "We're actually moving to LA?"

"If it's what you want."

"I think... yeah. Yes," she laughed. "I'd really like that."

Caressing her cheek, I tugged at her lower lip with my teeth. "I've loved you since the moment I knew you, Pet."

She brushed her own mouth, tracing where I'd touched. Her eyes were half shut.

"Once I knew who you were... *really were,* I fell in love with you, too."

Our experiences had been so different. And still, so similar.

Broken people shouldn't fit together with anyone. Our pieces are wrong, we can't mesh, and if you try to force us, we'll just damage the rest of the puzzle.

But when I'd met Alexis, darkening her life, I'd also darkened mine. Together, we'd become each others source of light. I could say without a doubt in the foundation of my soul, that there had never been a love like ours. It was the kind that came from pain, from fear, from destruction.

Only true love could have survived such torment.

And only true love could have won over my ruined heart...

While also healing hers.

Thanks for reading!

ABOUT THE AUTHOR

A USA Today Bestselling Author, Nora Flite loves to write dark romance (especially the dramatic, gritty kind!) Her favorite bad boys are the ones with tattoos, the intense alpha types that make you sweat and beg for more!

Inspired by the complicated events and wild experiences of her own life, she wants to share those stories with her audience. Born in the tiniest state, coming from what was essentially dirt, she's learned to embrace and appreciate every opportunity the world gives her.

She's also, possibly, addicted to coffee and sushi.

Not at the same time, of course.

Check out her website, noraflite.com, or email her at noraflite@gmail.com if you want to say hello! Hearing from fans is the best!

CPSIA information can be obtained at www.ICGtesting.com
Printed in the USA
BVOW02s1407240416

445421BV00033B/613/P